INCLINATIONS

by the same author

Vainglory (1915)
Inclinations (1916)
Odette: A Fairy Tale for Weary People (1916)
Caprice (1917)
Valmouth (1919)
The Princess Zoubaroff (1920)
Santal (1921)
The Flower Beneath the Foot (1923)
Sorrow in Sunlight (1924)
Concerning the Eccentricities of Cardinal Pirelli (1926)
The Artificial Princess (1934)
The New Rythum and other pieces (1962)

INCLINATIONS

by

RONALD FIRBANK

ADELAIDE
MICHAEL WALMER
2014

Inclinations first published 1916
This edition published 2014

by

Michael Walmer
49 Second Street
Gawler South
South Australia 5118

ISBN 978-0-9924220-1-1 paperback

＊

ERRATA
This edition has been prepared utlizing a previous edition; thus errors have been
reproduced. On page 120, line 21, for *Anne* please read *Arne*.
On page 124, line 18, for *curaçoa* please read *curaçao*.

PART I

"*Besides, I never ventured once to carry you with me to any conference I had with the Pope for fear you should be trying some of your coquettish airs upon him.*"—Lady Kitty Crockodile to Miss Lydell.

I

"'Hair almost silver—incredibly fair: a startling pallor.'" Otherwise, unmistakably, there was a close resemblance.

It is true, whenever she began a new work she said the same.

There were the Ducquelin, the Pizzi, the Queen Quickly periods . . . and that curious autumn evening when she had experienced the impulse of an old and wicked Cæsar. . . .

"And here am I rusting in Yorkshire!" she exclaimed.

In the twilight her face showed vague and indistinct: an earring gleamed.

"I adore your patience!"

"She seems to have had eleven children."

"Who, dear?"

"Mrs. Kettler. Catherine. Kitty."

"I wonder you don't get tired of going just on and on."

"My dear, you're always wondering."

"But now that Effie has begun her Tuesdays——"

"So often the mood only takes me as the gong sounds for dinner."

Viola Neffal moved her lips as if she were counting.

"Well, that Mortlake tapestry," she said, "pierced with nails and overhung by mirrors, is enough to make one weep!"

The Biographer clasped nervously her long, expressive hands.

"I sometimes think," she ventured, "that Modern things, rightly chosen, accentuate the past."

7

Through the open windows, a line of trees, leaning all one way, receded across the garden like figures escaping from a ball.

" Who was that woman, dear, who put her lover's head into a pot of basil? "

" You mean Isabel. But nothing shall ever dissuade me! Besides, after Princess Orvi I need a change. Two Italian women . . ."

Miss Neffal sprayed herself liberally with " Lethe Incarnate."

" . . . Here's luck! " she wished.

" Somehow I feel it may be a failure. I saw the new moon with my left eye."

" You never told me quite what there is to admire in Mrs. Kettler. Why she attracts you."

" It's hard to explain. . . . As a man of rare weight once remarked, she was like some radiant milkmaid."

" Are milkmaids so radiant as a rule? "

" She was. And then she was so English! Even from her earliest utterance: ' I would worship,' she said, ' to spend a summer in a hut in a hollow of Old Sarum.' She was then barely two."

" She appears to have been a gipsy."

" After all, very little about her is known! There's not much material. Hers was one of those flickering shadow-lives. . . . You catch her in flashes. In her hey-day she is said to have grown weary of her world and gone to Ceylon."

" *Ceylon?* "

" Well, if it wasn't Ceylon—— With these constant changes one is bound to get mixed. I'm not sure if it wasn't Greece. I've an idea it was Athens! "

" At any rate she was insular."

" Soul is as rare as radium."

Miss Neffal revealed her mind.

" The persons whom I should most have cared to meet were Walpole and Sappho," she said.

" If you aren't contented now you never will be! "

" That's vain."

" I was referring only to Hugh."

" Hugh! I am marrying him, Geraldine, as you know, mainly for his conversation. And of course I shall be very glad to be married. . . ."

" My dear Viola."

" When one is nearing the *end* of the twenties——"

" Nonsense! "

" Tell me more about the little milkmaid."

" Oh, well, very soon, now, I hope to be setting out again on my travels. I intend making a fairly extensive trip in *her* footsteps."

" You're off to Greece? "

" I'm going wherever she went."

" Perhaps you'll wander round by Cannes! "

Geraldine O'Brookomore, the authoress of *Six Strange Sisters*, *Those Gonzagas*, etc., unlocked a sombre lacquer case: a work of art, in its way, with its many painted labels all on tinted pearl.

" Reminiscences. Anecdotes. Apologias. Crimes. Follies. Fabrications. Nostalgia. Mysticism. Trivia. Human Documents. Love Letters. His to Me: Mine to Him," she read.

" It's Nostalgia you need. . . ."

Miss O'Brookomore raised her eyes.

" I'm sure I'm willing to hope so."

" Isn't it difficult often to be impartial? "

" It depends so much upon one's health. When one is tired a little or below par——"

" How I wish you were more sensible. *Is* it wise when the gong goes——"

" I know. But Effie spoils me. . . . Only a moment ago she sent me a peach that tasted like a dark carnation. . . ."

" Effie overdoes her hospitality I somehow think.

9

Placing rouge in all the bedrooms. Even in Mr. Fairmile's room, poor boy! "

" Who is there downstairs? "

" Such gold-wigged Botticellis—playing bridge. They've sent me up to look for you."

" For me? "

" To watch them."

" I won't. Because where would be the good? "

" Then they'll come trooping here instead. After dinner it's usually Effie's way to take a candle and drag everybody to gaze at the children in bed and asleep."

" Here comes someone now! "

" Were I to look in should I bother, weary, worry you? "

" It's Miss Collins."

" Mabel! "

" I've been waiting for you ever so long. This is quite the dullest house——"

" You poor little dreary cat! "

Miss Collins, who had never gone out before, seemed to believe a soirée to be a succession of bons-mots, songs and bursts of laughter.

" One should try to be happy always! "

" I suppose you'll say it's silly, but I want so much to l-i-v-e! I want to go flitting about the world like you."

Miss O'Brookomore became pensive.

" My work," she said, " lies largely among the dead."

" Is it imperative? "

" The worst of modern biography, you understand, is, one is never quite sure to what one is entitled——"

" If only to avoid the pitiful consequences," Miss Neffal theorised, " we should go through the world neatly and compact."

Miss Collins turned from her, oppressed.

" Effie sends a fresh supply of fruit. She is coming up very soon to look at the children."

" Raspberries! "

" Are there raspberries in Chaldea? "

" You astonish me! Why do you ask? "

" For information. Naturally, living continually in the same place——"

" Do you never go away? "

" From home? Oh yes . . . Sometimes, in winter, we go to Scotland."

" Surely Scotland in winter would be a desolation! Stone, and slate, and asphalt, and the wrong red hair. . . ."

" You see, we cannot get rid of our house."

" Indeed. And why not? "

" Because it stands in a valley. Although, of course, at times one gets some surprising effects of mist. . . ."

Miss Neffal leaned back in her chair with listless arms and fingers interlaced.

" Why attack the scenery? " she inquired.

Miss Collins shuddered.

" All that waving green," she said, " before the windows. . . . Why, the Chase looks haunted even in the sun."

" Poor child! "

" You've no conception. . . . I assure you there isn't a creature in all the countryside to interest one except, perhaps, Madame La Chose, who's an actress, although she has nothing to do with the stage."

" How can one be an actress without anything to do with the stage? " the Biographer wondered, drawing Miss Collins to her.

But Miss Collins did not seem to know.

" I love that ripple in your throat," she said. " It isn't a second chin. It's just a . . . ripple! "

" Mrs. Kettler had the same."

" Are you perpetually pondering your great men? "

" Naturally, those in hand."

" Often they muſt haunt you."

Miss O'Brookomore smiled.

" Occasionally," she said, " they do. In my dream laſt night I seemed to hear all those whose lives I've lately written moaning and imploring me not. Let the editions die, one good woman said to me. Let them be cancelled! "

" Ingratitude! "

" Dreams, have you never heard, go by *contraries*."

" Still, I'm sure you muſt need a change."

" Am I getting cloddish? "

" Quite otherwise."

" Once again in a *wagon-lit*——"

Miss Collins slipped to her knees.

" What would I not give," she said, " to go with you ! "

Slightly ſtartled, Miss O'Brookomore took from a cardboard box a cigarette.

" Supposing . . ."

" . . . supposing? "

" Supposing—I only say ' supposing '—supposing you were to accompany me to Greece. . . ."

Sparkling, Miss Collins rose.

" Only at the thought," she cried, " I could clap my feet in the air."

The Biographer considered her. Dark againſt the brilliance.

" My chief amusement," she explained, " has always been to exchange ideas with someone. And to receive new ones in return."

" At Corinth! . . ."

" At Aulis! "

" At Athens! "

" At Epidauros! "

" At Mycenæ! "

" In Arcadia! "

" It would be like a fairy dream."

" So long as you're good-humoured and sunny! "

" They say I'm rather silly sometimes at home."

Miss O'Brookomore dropped a sigh.

" Few of us are born mellow," she declared.

Miss Collins sank again to the floor.

" I suppose we should stifle all our emotions," she said. " And hide things. . . . But I never do. I just let my heart speak. And so——"

" I'm reading Lady Cray's *Travels*," Miss Neffal broke in. " ' In the desert,' she says, ' once, I tried to cook a partridge with a string, but the fire burnt the string and the partridge——' "

" Better to be foolish at home than——"

" Here's Effie! "

Candlestick in hand, and quite alone, their hostess appeared at the door.

" I knocked, but could get no answer! "

" I never heard you."

" Wild, interesting woman! Have you been doing *much?* "

" Not a great deal. One's best work is always unwritten."

" What she needs most," Miss Neffal reflected, " is the forsaken wing of a palace."

" Are you coming, Viola, to look at the children? "

" Dare I, I wonder, in these shoes. . . ."

" Is there anything wrong with them? "

" They might wake little Phillis. . . ."

" In any case, Mrs. Orangeman, I fancy, is destined to do that."

" . . . You hear her sad mind when she sings! "

Miss Collins looked shrewd.

" Her worries aren't enough," she prophesied, " to keep her going. . . ."

" Unless you are more careful," Miss Neffal threatened, " I will write you down in my *Book of Cats*."

" Have you kept it long? "

" Since I became engaged."

Their hostess tittered.

" Even we! . . ." she said. " Usually now on a dull day Jack likes to touch up his will."

" Doesn't it make you *nervous?* "

" Why should it? "

" I'd be afraid of his painting me out."

" That's because you're over highly strung. When people are pale and tired like you they need a rest."

" Well, I've finished almost for to-night. Perhaps I may come down presently when the curate's gone. The last time we met he referred to poor Kettler as a Hospital Case. . . ."

" Have you no sketch of her at all that we could see? "

" Only a replica. The original, if I recollect, is in the Liechtenstein Gallery."

And with her long and psychic fingers Miss O'Brookomore smoothed out a scroll.

" As a portrait," she said, " of course, it's a miracle of badness. But I think her face is so amusing and so alight."

Miss Collins gazed at the likeness sadly.

"I've seen so few good pictures," she lamented; " although an artist did come one autumn to Bovonorsip. He took a room at the Wheat Sheaf and trespassed all day at the Chase."

" Some artists can be very insinuating."

" So was he! It was impossible not to share this man's joy when he said he had captured a whole mood with a little grey paint. . . . 'Do not be too anxious to be like Corot, young ladies,' he would say when we went sketching too. And before he left he gave me a little wood scene with naked peasants."

Her hostess took up her torch.

" Poor Mr. Fairmile seems so miserable, Mabel, since you've disappeared! "

" How is he to show what he feels when——"

" When? "

" Oh, Effie, why did you tempt him? . . ." Miss Collins asked as she darted out.

" I wonder at anyone sitting down to pen the life of a woman so baggy about the eyes! " Miss Neffal exclaimed, returning the engraving.

" . . . Hark to Mrs. Orangeman. Well, Viola, will you come? "

Alone, Miss O'Brookomore wandered leisurely to the window and leaned out.

Beneath her a landscape all humming with little trees stretched away towards such delicate, merest hills.

" Was it solely Vampirism that made me ask her," she queried, " or is it that I'm simply bored? "

She looked up.

There was a suggestion of azalea in the afterglow that recalled to her the East.

" Either way," she murmured, " her mother most likely would never consent."

And seating herself before her mirror she began an examination of her raspberries for fear of little worms.

" When people are pale and tired like you . . ." had not Effie said?

She paused to dream.

How it tallied with Kate Kettler's description:

" Hair almost silver—incredibly fair: a startling pallor. . . ."

II

A BEEHIVE in Brompton, a tray of gleaming fish, the way the wind blew—everything that morning seemed extraordinarily Greek.

As Miss O'Brookomore made her way towards Harrods she rejoiced.

Miss Collins actually was in town!

" Take her and keep her," Mrs. Collins somewhat unexpectedly wrote. " Who better than Miss O'Brookomore could break my child of her tomboy habits? Athens, I imagine, must be a sweet spot. Those glorious noses! Fancies fade, but a portrait of Byron on horseback," etc.

And now, as Miss O'Brookomore strolled along, for some reason or other she screwed up her eyes and smiled.

All about her in heroic strips of green showed pastoral plots. Dark shrubberies. . . .

" Of course she will need a few new frocks," she mused, pausing before a—" Robes—Artistic Equipments "—at the corner of Ygdrasil Street, from whose folding doors at that same moment stepped the famous Mrs. Asp.

The veteran Biographer held out a hand.

" Your extensive acquaintance," she said, " I fear, has almost destroyed you for myself! They told me you had gone."

" I shall be leaving town now in about a week."

" Are you to be alone? "

" I shall have a maid—and a little Miss Collins, who is not yet fifteen."

Mrs. Asp began to purr.

" Should you need a really reliable maid," she said,
" I could tell you of an excellent woman. Nine weeks
with a Mrs. Des Pond and two . . . A treasure! Or,
should you be requiring a becoming blouse, or an
eerie hat, or anything . . . Mrs. Manwood in there
. . . It would be a charity! Silly thing . . . She
put all her money on Quiet Queenie, or was it Shy
Captain, and lost. . . ."

" For my journey," Miss O'Brookomore said, with
a glance of concern, " I shall take with me only what
is most serviceable and neat, and absolutely austere."

" My dear, you will allow me, I hope, to know as
much about travelling as you do. I expect I have been
abroad as many times as you have."

" Rumours, no doubt, have reached you of my
present choice? "

Mrs. Asp became faintly asthmatic.

" How hugely, purely, curiously and *entirely* reckless
one's disciples are. . . ."

" Naturally, I shall suggest poor Kitty's cynicisms
with fairy lightness . . . in fact——"

" To me," Mrs. Asp said, " Mrs. Kettler has always
made her appeal. . . . And when you're in Athens
you should go to Tanagra—not that there's very
much there to see."

Miss O'Brookomore held up an arm.

" If I'm late at all," she observed, " I shall miss
Miss Collins . . . or keep her waiting, perhaps, about
the street. One can hardly credit it, but she has never
been away from home before! "

" Well, even when I was still seventeen I would
take my skipping-rope into the Park. . . ."

" I should like to have seen you."

" We have a wee box in the third tier at the opera
for to-night if you would care to come! "

" This evening we are going to the Dream Theatre,
and can't. . . . Besides, I've an aversion for Covent

Garden, I fear. One sits in a blaze of light, looking eighty, or ninety, or a hundred—as the case may be."

Mrs. Asp nodded.

" I shall expect to hear from you," she said, " at any rate, quite soon. An Athenian husband for you both . . . a villa each in Thrace. . . . I could wish for nothing more! And now, as the Oratory is so near, I feel tempted almost to run in. Although, as a rule, I never care to go to Confession in anything that's *tight*."

And there, in front of Harrods, teasing a leashed dog with a requirements-list, stood Miss Collins.

" Let us make haste," Miss O'Brookomore said, saluting her somewhat nervously, "to do our shopping. And afterwards, just to break the ice, I intend to take you to an Oriental restaurant in Soho. . . ."

III

"It's funny," Miss Collins said, "but even the most trivial things amuse me now I'm away from home!"

"Your strong *joie de vivre*," Miss O'Brookomore informed her, "your youthfulness, already have done me good."

"Tell me whom you see."

"Hardly one's ideal. On the couch, half asleep, are Guarini and Ozinda. Pirouetting round them, making their survey, is Lord Horn and the Misses Cornhill, and on the dais there's January, Duchess of Dublin, and her Doxy."

"Which is Doxy?"

"In tears. At galleries she's quite dreadful. She will begin to weep almost for the Spinario's ' poor foot.'"

"Once while beagling, accidentally——"

There came a murmur of voices.

". . . terrifying nightmare women."

". . . One of his wild oats."

". . . fascinating, fiendish colours."

"It's unmistakably *his*."

"Pish!"

"Take me away!"

"And behind us," Miss O'Brookomore chimed in, "Lady Betty Benson is being escorted by a tenth son and a real murderer, and in ambush by the door, chatting to Miss Neffal's fiancé, is Mrs. Elstree, the actress."

"O-o-o-o-h!"

"You have the catalogue."

"What should you say it was?"

19

"Dear old Mr. Winthrop! He's so vague always—
'Sunrise India.' And I know for a fact it was painted
in his street. Those trees are in Portman Square."

"Is not that Miss O'Brookomore? We heard that
you had gone."

Miss O'Brookomore turned slightly.

"We are in Ospovat's hands," she murmured,
"still."

"Have you chosen yet your route?"

"We go from Marseilles to the Piræus, and from
there we take the tram."

"O-o-o-o-h!"

"You have the catalogue."

". . . know Mr. Hicky?" Mrs. Elstree was be-
ginning to scream. "Why, when I was playing in the
Widow of Wells I died in his arms every night for over
a year."

"Hugh, where's Viola?"

"I'm afraid I must decline to tell you."

"Indeed! . . ."

"I left her burning *Zampironi* before a Guardi and
invoking Venice."

"Anything later than the eighteenth century I
know how she dislikes."

Mrs. Elstree addressed the Historian.

"Daring one," she murmured, "I admire you
more than you're aware of! You're simply never
trite."

"You mean my Mrs. Kitty? . . ."

"And even should you not discover much, failure
makes one subtler!"

"All I hope to get's a little glamour."

"Once—did I ever tell you?—I rented a house in
Lower Thames Street, where the Oyster Merchants
are."

Miss O'Brookomore closed her eyes.

"When I was quite a child," she said, "I did not

20

care for sweets . . . but I liked Oysters. Bring me Oysters, I would say. I want Oysters."

" Poet."

Miss Collins folded herself together as though for a game of hide-and-seek.

" Really, Mabel! Noting you with dismay is Mrs. Felicity Carrot of *Style*."

" A reporter! "

" One should be the spectator of oneself always, dear, a little."

" Don't move—I am not sure but I see my aunt! "

" Your aunt? "

" Mrs. Hamilton-of-Hole."

" . . . My husband's horizons are solely political ones," Mrs. Hamilton was explaining as she elbowed by.

" And there is Mr. Winthrop, whose landscape——"

Mrs. Elstree moved away.

" Ozinda has fallen sound asleep in Guarini's arms! . . ."

There came a confusion of voices.

" Babes-in-the-Wood."

" We think of crossing over to witness the autumn at Versailles."

" . . . goes to auctions."

" The slim, crouching figure of the Magdalen is me."

" Those break-neck brilliant purples."

" Pish! "

" A scarlet song."

" ' Order what you please from Tanguay,' he said —' a tiara, what you please.' "

" ——You'd think they'd been set by Bœhmer! "

" O-o-o-h! "

" You have the catalogue."

" Mrs. Elstree took it with her."

" LET us all cling together! "

Miss O'Brookomore blinked her eyes.

" Is it a Station? "

" To-morrow," Miss Collins announced from behind her chronicle, ignoring the sleep-murmurings
of the Historian's maid, " six Cornish girls are to dance
at the Lune Grise. What a pity to have missed them.
Although I believe I mind more about Mona. When
she discovers I've been in Paris without even trying
to find her——"

" Who is that, dear? "

" Napier's sister—Mr. Fairmile's. Oh, Gerald! "

" What is it? "

" Mr. Fairmile and I once . . . Yes, dear! We're
engaged. . . . And when he said good-bye he didn't
kiss me. He just crushed me to his heart. . . ."

" Crushed you? "

" My frock a little. One of Miss Johnson's jokes."

" That white one? "

" Of course Mona I've known always. She's just
a dear. Tall, with a tiny head. And such beautiful,
mystic hands. . . . She and I were at school together."

" I didn't know you had ever been at school."

" . . . a Term. She was quite my bosom-chum at
York Hill. Once we exchanged a few drops of each
other's blood. Oh, Gerald! "

" Really! "

" It was on a certain Sunday in June."

Miss O'Brookomore dropped the fireproof curtain
across her eyes. She glazed them.

" I think I shall tuck up my feet," she said, " and lie down."

" Just as there's a sunset coming on? "

" I'm tired. My head aches. My mind has been going incessantly all day. . . ."

Miss Collins showed her sympathy.

" Reading in the train would upset anyone," she observed. " I'm sure it would me."

" I was renewing my acquaintance with the classics."

" Before I came away mum made me get by heart a passage from *The Queen of Tartary* to recite to you the instant we landed, as a surprise. You know the great tirade! The Queen has taken the poison and leaves the Marquee on her confidante's arm. Inside, the banquet is in full swing. Now and again you can hear their hearty laughter. . . . Ha, ha, ha! Ha, ha, ha, ha! And the Queen turns to Melissa—and mum declares she shall never forget the impression Madam Dolce Naldi made as the Queen, although Miss Faucet, as Melissa, was exquisite in her fragility as a foil—and says: ' My hands are cold. It's as if my eyelids had weights upon them. . . . I hear a singing in my ears. I feel,' etc. And so on through the greater part of the medical dictionary."

" It's curious your mother did not select the triumphal speech. Act II, Scene 3: ' Everybody crowded round me, . . .' " Miss O'Brookomore remarked.

" I don't know. The only books I care for are those about Farms."

" My dear, when one speaks of Farms one forgets the animals. Little piggy-wiggs. . . ."

" I don't think that *that* would matter."

" Perhaps some day, when you marry a country squire, you will have a farm of your own."

" It isn't likely. Before leaving town I consulted a clairvoyant. There are indications, she said, that something *very disgraceful* will come about between January and July."

" Oh, Mabel! "

Miss Collins reached towards a bag of sweets.

" In the crystal she could see mum reading my letters . . . she could see her, she said, on all fours hunting about. . . ."

" Your poor mother."

" What's the good of grieving? "

" Mab dear, you're always nibbling! "

" To beguile the time."

" But so bad for you."

" Beware of a dazzlingly fair man, the woman said. Beware of him. And in the end, after many petty obstructions, which you will overcome, she said, you'll marry a raven! "

Miss O'Brookomore became attentive to the scenery.

To watch the trees slip past in the dusk was entrancing quite. In a meadow a shepherdess with one white wether stood up and waved her crook.

" Poor Palmer seems completely worn out."

The maid stirred slightly at her name.

" When Greek meets Greek, miss," she asked informingly, "can you tell me what they're supposed to do? "

" Since we're all English," Miss O'Brookomore replied, " I don't think it matters. . . ."

Miss Collins covered her face with a soiled *suède* glove.

" Another tunnel! "

" You should really rest, Mab. You'll arrive so tired."

" I'm that already. But I won't lean back—for fear of contracting something . . infectious."

" Some day, dear, I may arrange your sayings in a wreath. . . ."

" Our coachman once——"

24

" No, please—I'm altogether incurious."

" Although, even bolt upright, dear, I can sleep as easily as a *prima donna* upon a dais! Nothing wakes me."

Palmer raised an eye towards the waning moon.

" The evenings," she remarked, " turn quite bleak. Had I known, I'd not have come away without my bit of fur."

V

" AND then we almoſt ran. Anybody would have said
our husbands were behind. . . . And perhaps they
pitied us. But Miss O'Brookomore's so unpunctual
always; it's a marvel we ever catch a train."

He waved a hand.

" Those talents! That gift! Her mind! "

" At Marseilles we even missed the boat. Otherwise, very likely, we would have never met."

" M-a-b-e-l," Miss O'Brookomore called.

Miss Collins turned.

" Do you need me, dear? "

" Who is your handsome friend? "

" He's . . . Oh, Gerald! "

" Where did you pick him up? "

" He began by speaking of the tedium of water for
a sailor, and then——"

" I see! "

" Oh, Gerald, it's Count Paſtorelli. . . ."

Miss O'Brookomore leaned back a little in her
deck-chair.

" Take my word for it," she said, " he's not so
paſtoral as he sounds."

" And there's another! "

" You mean——? "

" A porpoise! "

Miss O'Brookomore crossed herself.

" I always do," she said, " when anyone points."

" Shall we take a little prowl? "

" Voluntarily."

" There's a person on board, someone perhaps
should speak to her, who sits all day ſtaring at the sea

26

beneath a very vivid violet veil. And when the waves break over her she never even moves. . . ."

The Biographer watched sagaciously the sun touch the dark water into slow diamonds.

" One should blur," she observed, " the agony."

Miss Collins became evidently intellectual.

" Which would you prefer," she inquired, " a wedding or a funeral out at sea? "

" I'd prefer there was no unpacking."

" For the one emergency I've enough, of course, of white . . . and for the other, I dare say I could lean from the ship-side in a silver hat crowned with black Scotch roses."

" Were it mine, I'd give that hat to Palmer."

" Poor thing, every time the ship rolls she seems to hear something say: *The captain—his telescope.*"

" She will see the land very soon now with her naked eye."

Miss Collins slipped an arm about her friend.

" I look forward first to eleven o'clock," she said, " when the ship-boy goes round with bananas."

" Tell me, at Bovonorsip does every one speak so loud? "

Miss Collins clicked her tongue.

" Shall we go down upon the lower-deck, Gerald, and look through the cabin windows? There's the Negress you called a *Gaugin*. . . . All alone in her cabin it would be interesting to see what she does. . . ."

" Somehow I'd sooner save that poor veiled thing from getting wet."

But that " poor veiled thing " was enjoying herself, it appeared.

" . . . I don't object to it, really," she said. " I rather like the sea! . . . I'm Miss Arne. Mary Arne —the actress. Some people call me their Mary Ann, others think of me as Marianne."

" The tragedienne."

27

" Comedy is my province. I often say I'm the only Lady Teazle! "

" Then of course you've met Lizzie Elstree? "

" . . . I can recall her running about the green-room of the Garden Theatre in I should be afraid to say quite what. . . ."

" Well, I always hate to hustle."

Miss Collins nodded.

" There's the Count," she exclaimed. " He will keep bumping into me."

" I wonder who he can be."

" I believe he's a briefless barrister."

Miss O'Brookomore looked wary.

" How is one to tell? " she murmured. " He may *not* be so briefless . . . ! "

" I know nothing about the law," Miss Arne said. " Although when I played in *The Coronation of Lucy* there was a trial scene that lasted nearly forty minutes."

" You must be delighted now to rest."

"Rest! I'm on my way to Greece to study Lysistrata."

" But couldn't you have done it at home? "

" Not with the same results. As I told the silly critics, I mean to treat her as a character-part."

" I understand. When one traces a shadow it's mostly for the scenery."

" At Cape Sunium," Miss Collins said, " I shall lie like a starfish all day upon the sand."

" My dear, at Sunium there is no sand. It's all rocks."

" How do you know there are rocks? "

" Do you think I haven't seen old engravings? "

" Perhaps I might paddle."

" ' Oh! joy, joy! no more helmet, no more cheese nor onions! ' " Miss Arne soliloquised.

" I adore Aristophanes."

" Certainly, he has a flavour——"

Miss Arne stood up.

" What can that be over there? "
" Those slopes. . . ."
" These villas. . . ."
" And temples. . . ."
" It must be . . ."
" It is——"
Miss Collins commenced a feverish country dance.
" It's Athens! "

VI

" So far I've not observed one! "

" Of what? "

" A nose! Athens and heavenly noses. . . . Mum said I should."

Miss O'Brookomore threw upon her head a bewildering affair with a vampire-bat's-wing slanting behind.

" Patience," she murmured. " We haven't been here long enough."

" Quite long enough to find out the English chemist isn't English! "

" Why, aren't you up to the mark? "

" I was attempting to ward off freckles."

" Pretty Mrs. Wilna often used to say the utmost she ever did was to apply a little cold-cream *just* as she got into bed."

Miss Collins moved from one chair to another.

" Oh, come and look! Oh!"

" What ever is it? "

" There's such a shocking dispute in the Square! "

Beneath a bruised blue, almost a violet, sky lay the town. Very white and very clean.

On the pavement some youths, with arms entwined, seemed to be locked in the convulsions of a dance.

" Let us go down and sit in a café."

Miss O'Brookomore became evasive.

" I want you to repress yourself a little for a few days. Be more discreet."

" Because——"

" Professor and Mrs. Cowsend have the rooms next ours. . . ."

" Buz! Let them! "

" Also, the Arbanels are here on their honeymoon.
. . . You never saw such ghosts on their rambles."

" Who is Mr. Arbanel? "

" He's very blasé."

Miss Collins clasped her hands.

" I'd give almost anything to be blasé."

Miss O'Brookomore turned from her.

" Those Customs! " she lamented. " Everything
arrives so *crushed*."

" Are you going out to see what you can find? "

" I dare say I may look in at the library of the
University."

Miss Collins became contemplative.

" Who knows, away in the Underworld she may
be watching you. . . . "

" My poor puss, Athens must seem to you a trifle
dull."

" It isn't really. I could sit for hours on my balcony
and watch the passers-by. So many of them don't pass.
At least, not directly."

" You mean they stop? "

" Sometimes. But what does it matter?—when
one isn't a linguist."

" Palmer should be with you more."

" Palmer seems so squeamish."

The Biographer fetched a sigh.

" Indeed, the way she sprinkles naphthaline has
quite put out the violets."

" All except her own! "

" Her own? "

" Oh, Gerald. . . . Every week there is a dance,
dear, in the hotel."

Miss O'Brookomore shrugged her shoulders.

" Don't expect me to attend any of them," she said,
" that's all."

" Oh, darling, how can you be so Spartan! How? "

" You forget, dear, my dancing days are nearly done."

" Wait. . . . Wait. . . . *Wait* till you hear the throb-thrum-throb of a string band. . . . Oh, Gerald!"

" I should be sound asleep."

" Fiddlesticks! You'd fling a wrap about you and down you'd come."

" It's true."

" And you'd heighten your cheeks in such a hurry that everybody would suppose you'd been using jam."

" Believe me, I'd deal with the manager without the least compunction."

" You'd complain? "

" I'd demand to change my room."

" S-s-s-h! Here's Palmer."

" Ah, no more naphthaline, please."

" There's a packet for Miss Hill. . . ."

" Take it away. It's not for us."

" I expect it's for me! Collins, Colline, Collina *Hill*. I thought it was advisable not to give my own name at any of the shops. . . ."

" Collina! Have you been chatting with the Count?"

" As I went out he was stirring up the weather-glass in the front hall."

" I fear he takes you to be an heiress."

" But he's very well off as it is! Haven't you noticed? He doesn't tip. He *rewards*. Besides, dear, I could never marry a man who had corns on his feet, or who didn't say his prayers."

" How do you know he has corns? "

" Because he told me. He couldn't get up to the Acropolis, he said, on account of his corns. . . ."

" Isn't that a blessing? "

" Look, Gerald, I bought these tags to keep off flies."

" In Arcadia they will be just the thing."

" The Count was saying how rash it was for two docile women to go alone into such inaccessible places. . . ."

With pursed lips the Historian tuned her veil.

" Pooh! " she fiddled.

VII

" And when papa's reverse of fortune did come . . .
why, then, of course, I thought of *everything* . . . to
be a maid, I thought. . . . To look up at the moon
through the palings. . . . But somehow, no! I
couldn't. . . ."

" . . . Shall we have our coffee in the lounge? "

" The night is wonderful," a woman with a thrilling
voice declared.

" Evening here is really the nicest time! "

In an alcove, unable to contain her laughter, Miss
Collins was teaching English versicles to the Count.

" The naked oak-tree in the deer-park stands
   Mocking the brooding moose."

" Dear? "

" *D-e-e-r!* "

" Oh, my dear! "

" *Hinds! . . . Deer!* "

" I adore you, dear."

" *Harts!* "

" Our two hearts! "

" Mabel! Miss O'Brookomore called."

" Oh, Gerald, what ever is it? "

" Come and thank Mrs. Cowsend. . . . She has
consented to take you out occasionally when I'm
engaged."

" I shall be delighted," Mrs. Cowsend said. " To-
morrow we intend to pass the morning in the royal
gardens."

" Unfortunately I'm not overfond of flowers.

34

Gardening in the rain was one of our punishments at home."

" But at the palace there are so few flowers. Scarcely any! It's bays a bit, and cypress a bit, and ilex a little, and laurel a lot, with here and there an oleander, perhaps, or a larch. . . . Nothing that could remind you! "

" The very sight of a wheelbarrow quite upsets me."

" Personally, I'm inclined to worship a wheel-barrow. It makes a change with the temples."

Miss O'Brookomore became introspective.

" To visit Greece with Professor Cowsend," she said, " would be *my* idea of happiness. . . ."

" My dear Miss O'Brookomore, I have found things in Somerset just as lovely as in the Vale of Tempe. And with none of the fatigue."

The Historian held up a map.

" Where we are going," she announced, " is dotted white."

" You must be very careful! . . . It's just the region——"

Miss O'Brookomore stiffened.

" Tell me everything," she begged.

" I dare say you've not encountered a sheep-dog here before? Some of them are so fierce. More like wolves."

" And dogs frequently fly at me! "

" Round Delphi they are quite dreadful. Parnassos, I assure you, is literally overrun. . . ."

" Dogs delight to lick me," Miss Collins said, " when they get the chance. . . ."

With a lorgnon Mrs. Cowsend drummed the map.

" At Megara," she said, " there is a calvary to commemorate one of the Seymoures. But of course Lady Maisie attracted attention by her peplum even in the town."

" I'm told the measles in Athens just now is very bad."

" Even so, I must say, I find the city dull. Mr. Cowsend, you see, is continually out gathering notes for lectures. Often he will leave the hotel as soon as it is light and pass the entire day poking about the Pnyx. . . . And the shops for me. . . . Well, on the whole, I don't think much of them."

" I would take a camp-stool sometimes and sit on the Pnyx as well."

" . . . When I did the other day he didn't seem to like it! And, in any case, he never tells me much. I approach Greece by way of the Renaissance, and I don't pretend to know anything about either."

Miss O'Brookomore bowed amicably.

" Mrs. Arbanel to-night is really an Eastern dream. . . ."

" Her husband, it seems, is incredibly inattentive to her, poor dear."

" It seems a little soon."

" There's a boy in the porch selling strings and strings of amber," the lady murmured as she ambled by.

" Miss O'Brookomore has just been saying you could scarcely be more Zara or Turkish if you tried."

" How suggestive that is of chains! "

Miss O'Brookomore protested.

" With you," she said, " I only see the beads."

" We were wedded at St. Margaret's almost a month ago! "

" I read of your little adventure in the *Morning Post*."

" I forget if you know Gilbert at all. . . ."

" I can hardly say I know him, but I think we sat together once upon the same settee."

" Would it be lately? "

Mrs. Cowsend smiled urbanely.

36

" Absence or surfeit," she observed, " it seems there's nothing between."

" Although it *is* my honeymoon I'm not at all exacting."

Miss O'Brookomore used her fan.

" It's been such a heavenly day! "

" I spent most of it in a wood on the Marathon Road," Mrs. Arbanel said, " with *A Midsummer Night's Dream. . . .*"

" Hermia! Lysander! Oberon! Titania! Oh dear! " Miss Collins showed her culture.

" Bottom," she added.

" . . . I hate to sight-see. However, to-morrow, I'm told I must. Mr. Arbanel has engaged an open coach. . . . But, as I said to him, it would no longer be a coach. It would be a waggon. . . ."

" You should take a cab and drive to Eleusis. . . . On Sunday, I believe, it's the only thing to do."

Mrs. Arbanel looked bored.

" I've seen nothing here quite as delicate," she confessed, "as the Little Trianon in a shower of April rain."

Mrs. Cowsend twinkled.

" You should tell that to the Professor presently when he comes in."

" Where do the men tide through the evening? They invariably disappear."

" In the covered passage behind the hotel," Miss Collins said, " there's a Viennese beer hall and a picture palace. Oh, Gerald! "

" Mr. Cowsend after dinner usually goes to a café in the Rue d'Hèrmes and does dominoes."

" All alone! "

" Or with Professor Pappas—who's apt, on the whole, to be dull. When he was introduced he started off about the county of Warwick. Or the Countess of Warwick. And then he referred to Shakespeare."

37

Miss Arne turned.

" What is that about the stage? "

" Nothing," Miss Collins said.

" One of these days, Marianne, you should arrange a Lysistrata *matinée* upon the Acropolis."

" Boxes full. Stalls full. Gallery full. Pit full. *Standing-room only!* "

" Don't people stand at concerts? They promenade. . . ."

" I dare say."

" There is a girl in the corner over there watching you who'd make a rare Lampito. . . ."

" She is an Australian, poor thing, seeking her parents."

Miss O'Brookomore blinked.

" Well, she needn't start staring at me! "

" In certain lights," Miss Collins murmured, " she has a look of Edith Jackson, who was sacked from York Hill."

" Why, what had she done? "

" Oh, nothing very much."

" She must have done something."

" . . . She gave a dance in her bedroom—the *houla-houla!* But that wasn't *really* all. . . . Oh, good gracious! "

" To-morrow we shall have one here I expect in the hotel."

" Mr. Arbanel has composed a charming air expressly for it."

" My dear, how can one dance to his brain pictures? "

" Oh, listen! "

" When the wind breaks this way you can hear distinctly what they're saying in the café."

" Ta-lirra-lirra-lo-la-la.
  La-lirra-lirra-lo-la-la!
  Ta-lirra-lirra-lirra,
  La-lirra-lirra-lirra,
  Ta-lirra-lirra-lo-la-la! "

" It's politics! "
" It must be."
" Such optimism! "
" One does hope that Mr. Cowsend——"
Miss Collins drifted over to the Count.
" Deer—have you forgotten? . . ."
" Oh, the ' little dear '! "
" Mercy! "
" Another verse."
" Not now; I mustn't! "
" When shall I see you again? "
" To-morrow, I dare say, at the siesta hour—when
Miss O'Brookomore goes to her room for a snooze...."
He bent his head above her fingers.
" Good night, Miss Mabina. I kiss those charming
hands."
Miss Collins glanced at them.
" Mine? " she sighed.

VIII

Sardonic, she stirred the salad: tumbling, jostling, pricking, poking it, parting the trembling leaves. Pursuing a rosy radish, or . . .

" Oh, Gerald, everyone is watching you! . . ." unearthing the glaring eyes of eggs.

" Why begin throwing it about? "

Orchestrating olives and tomatoes, breaking the violet beetroot. . . .

" Oh, Gerald! "

. . . tracking provoking peas—scattering paprinka, pouring tarragon, dashing *huile*.

" Yoicks, dear! "

" Athenæus, you know, maintains a lettuce is calming to Love! "

" Who ever mentioned love? I only said I liked him dreadfully."

Miss O'Brookomore leaned her chin upon her hand: she rested.

" Where *is* this Pastorelli? " she asked. " I mean the town."

" It's a little way outside of Orvieto. Not very far from Rome."

" Really? Rome. . . ."

" Avid thing! I believe you long to be there."

" I see no reason to complain."

" Think of the countless persons who've never come to Greece." Then finding Worcester Sauce—

" It doesn't seem fair! "

Miss Collins looked sage.

" Such," she remarked, " is life! "

" You haven't told me, Mab, about Pastorelli yet.

. . . There's a cathedral with frescoes there, you say. Scuola di—*who?* A campo-santo. And what else? "

" There's the house, of course, where he was born. It stands beside such a wicked-looking lake, and the gardens sowed with statues. He showed me a photograph of his family seated in it. Oh, my gracious! "

" His family? "

" Just the natural blood ones. . . ."

" After *déjeuner* you should really write to your——"

" What's the good? . . . Mum's away in Edinburgh. She says she must try to content herself with *Modern Athens* as she doesn't suppose she shall ever see the other. So papa—poor old gentleman—is left all alone to look after my kiddy sister Daisy, who can neither read nor write. Mum won't let her be educated, she says, as it hasn't answered at all with me. And frequently, for a f-f-friend, she is asked to display her ignorance."

" Her what? "

" How you said it: What! I love Napier *best*, dear, always when he says, ' What.' W-h-a-t! What! Oh, Gerald, I can't explain. . . . You'll never know——"

" I do know. It's like the crack of a cart-whip. Exactly."

Miss Collins began eating crumbs at random.

" A whip? Oh, Gerald——"

" You seem to have entirely forgotten Napier since you've become interested in the Count."

" After all, what is he but a Yorkshire pudding? "

" Still, he's your fiancé! "

" Do look at the man exactly opposite. Doesn't he give you the impression rather of something torn up by the roots? "

" He obviously has a little money, and she is spending it! "

Miss Collins whisked her eyes over the room.

Midway along Mrs. Arbanel appeared to be absorbed in a vivacious and seemingly vital conversation with the *maitre d'hôtel*.

" I should love to seem so thoughtful! "

" I don't see Mrs. Cowsend, do you? "

" Breakfast was laid for four covers in her room."

" For four! "

" Or perhaps it was only three."

" Greece via the Renaissance would knock up most of us."

" Why, even the Tartary tirade———"

" Remember you owe me that."

" The library at Bovon, you know, is full of that sort of thing. . . . Although mum detests all serious books. She likes them frothy. Whenever she goes into York she's sure to come back with something smart."

" Hasn't the eccentricity of living near York ever occurred to your mother? "

"Oh, Gerald, it's dreadful for us all, dear, but what can we do if nobody takes the house? "

" There must be some way of getting rid of it."

" Mum's in Edinburgh now to see what can be done. She thinks some person perhaps pining for the South———"

" One never knows! "

" I'll read you her letter, shall I? There's a message too for you."

Miss O'Brookomore sipped listlessly her Château Décélée.

" ' My adored angel,' she says, ' my darling child, Mab. . . . If you knew how wretched I am without you!' Oh! . . . ' Couldn't you have got a *quieter* violet? . . .' She's interested too in Miss Arne! 'As Juliet,' she says, ' she was astonishing! Though one can't help feeling she has danced at the Empire. Crossing Princes Street I let fall the Ethiopian skin that I got from Mrs. Mattocks.' And she asks me to be

42

photographed in your . . . something . . . 'hat and
Zouave jacket and a bunch of violets on one shoulder.'
(Then she says, as I told you:) ' I must try to content
myself with Modern Athens,' she says, ' as I don't
suppose I shall ever see the Other. . . . Who should
I come across at the Caledonian but Sukey and Booboo.
They *were* so glad to find me here, and on Sunday we
all went together to hear Father Brown. He spoke to
us so simply, so eloquently, so touchingly that I quite
. . . Never forget, my pet, that . . .

" ' He reminds me just a little of St. Anthony of
Padua. . . . What is all this about *an Italian?* Oh,
Girlie. If ever we let the Chase we must persuade papa
to travel. . . .

" ' Listening lately to the Y.M.C.A. singing " There
is a Green Hill," I felt I wanted to take a taxi and
drive straight to it. Mum's picnic days are nearly over
now. . . . Soon it's *she* who'll be the ruin. Those
that care enough for her will toil to her bedside, perhaps, with their baskets, as they would to some de-
cayed, romantic tower—the Lermers, poor Nell Flint,
dear Mrs. Day—and they will sprawl upon her *causeuse*
and trot out their ginger beer. Doctors will try to
restore her, patch her up . . .

" ' But mum won't let them. She will just roll over
on one side and show them . . .' "

" And the message? "

" I'm coming."

" ' . . . and show them, as Dolce Naldi did, they
arrive *too late*. The prospect of another damp winter
——' "

" The message! "

" ' Give my kind regards to Miss O'Brookomore.' "

" She writes curiously in the style of one of my
unknown correspondents."

" She's full of trivial sadness."

" Scotland should do her good."

43

" What would you do, Gerald, if you were to look round and there was somebody in a kilt? "

Miss O'Brookomore blinked.

" I don't suppose I should do anything," she said.

" Oh wouldn't you? "

" I *might* . . ."

" Try one. . . . I don't know what they are; at school we called them French Madonnas."

" They look fairly rich, anyway."

" Once I ate nineteen méringues. . . ."

" Pig! "

" You've to eat a peck of dirt before you die, Gerald."

" Not if I know it."

" Give me a bit of the brown."

" What are your father's initials, in case I should write to him? "

" C. It's for Charles! . . . Poor old gentleman."

" You should answer your mother yourself. Promise her a photograph."

" On the night they draw the lottery there's to be a subscription ball at the opera."

" What has that to do with it? "

" It's to be in fancy dress."

" I understand."

" I thought we could be photographed in our dresses."

" I see."

" Oh, Gerald, you could be a silver-tasselled Portia almost with what you have, and I a Maid of Orleans."

" You! "

" Don't be tiresome, darling. It's not as if we were going in *boys'* clothes! "

" Really, Mabel——"

" Of course, it's as you like! "

" So that's settled."

" Oh, Gerald, for my sake subscribe."

44

" I subscribe? I subscribe! I subscribe nothing."

" When the Shire-Hall at home was blown away I helped to collect for the restorations. . . ."

Miss O'Brookomore pinned up her veil.

" After the siesta what do you propose to do? "

" I'm going out to do some shopping. I should like to buy a small piece of old pottery for Mrs. Elk, of York. You know she collects jars. And then our head housemaid asked me to lay out a few shillings on ' some very Greek-looking thing,' she said. And I mustn't forget the footman. . . ."

" What did he want? "

" A knife."

" You seem to have commissions for all the servants."

"At home, you see, dear, I nearly always use the back stairs . . . They're so much more interesting than the front ones . . . Once Daisy saw a soldier on them . . . He was going up! And another time——"

Miss O'Brookomore yawned.

" Mercy," she said, " the siesta-hour's upon us! "

I X

" No, there's really no resisting him. I'm sure there isn't. Who could? There's no resisting him at all—none. No. . . ."

Demurely she shed a shoe.

" I shouldn't care to be more in love than I am at present. No, indeed! Even if I could. . . ."

She sank slowly into bed.

" Oh, you silly creature!

" Love! O Lord!

" I shall never sleep. I don't see how I can. The die is cast! There's no telling, child, how it will end! . . .

". . . Via Tiber. . . . Countess P-a-s-t-o-r-e-l-l-i. Via Tiber. . . . ' O Tiber, Father Tiber, *to whom the Romans pray.*' Impossible! . . . If they did, it was a perfect scandal.

"And suppose he made me too? Oh, good gracious!"

By the bedside, mellowing among a number of vellum volumes, were the *Nine Prayers* of the Countess of Cochrane and Cray.

Who would do the burning?

That eighth one! What a clamour for a crown!

On the subject of jewels there wasn't much she didn't teach.

Two loose diamonds made a charming toc-toc sound.

At a dinner-party, now, who would work in first? She or Lady Cray? One would push past her probably, in any case—" the *Italian* woman! " . . . "*The Pasto* Countess thing! "

She played her eyes and flung out a hand towards a sugar-crystal-rose.

46

No; one couldn't exactly tell how it would end.
" My dear, I shouldn't care to say! . . ."
There were those Beer-Hall voices. . . . " Fal de
rol di do do, *di do do!* Fal de rol——"
Miss Collins turned her pillow.
" I suppose I've to lie and listen! . . . Oh, good
gracious! "

X

" ' I AM sure I always found her to be moſt induſtrious, clever, natty, and honeſt.' That was Mrs. Vernigan's. This is Miss Miser. And here is the Ex-Princess Thleeanouhee."

" Why bother Miss Palmer any more about it? I always say it's a lottery wherever one goes."

" Once," Mrs. Arbanel's maid declared, " I took a situation with a literary lady—the Scottish-Sappho. She wrote *Violet's Virtue*, or it might have been *The Virtue of Violet.*"

" Anyway! "

" Oh, for the wings of a dove."

" Come along, Miss Clint, now. It's not so far."

Before them the Acropolis, half hidden by thin clouds, showed like a broken toy.

" Naturally, one sees it has its old associations. . . ."

" I dare say. But to my mind it doesn't look half the age of the Abbey church at home. Now, that does look worn if you like."

" Worn, my dear, don't speak of being worn! "

Clint sighed.

" Whenever I'm lonely or depressed," she said, " or valeting anyone who's juſt a little wee bit . . . Well! I know there's only one thing for me to do. I take a taxi and go and sit in the church of St. Bartholomew the Great. It has a *je ne sais quoi* about it somehow that comforts me."

" It would give some people the dismals, dear."

" Well, I always leave when I'm annoyed! "

" ' Quick with her needle, an early riser, I am sure——' "

48

" Give them back to me."

" ' I am sure no hours are too *long* for her.' "

" It's what I should call the portrait of a slave."

" Where is Elizabeth? "

" I'm here."

" And Mademoiselle? "

" Lagging along behind."

Miss Clint made a gesture towards the Erechtheum.

" Come along, girls! " she called.

" Oh! I never knew Lot had six wives. . . ."

" Can't you see she's always the same? "

" Our previous butler was a widower. He seemed inconsolable."

" Sooner or later, we each of us bear our cross! . . . Where I lived last you might gather one of those downy-puffy things and, blowing, say: ' First footman, second footman, third footman, fourth footman . . . .' And if there was any down over ' Pantry-boy, page. . . .' "

" With the Jamjanets, of course, it was hotel-life half the time. Eating, drinking and dressing made up *their* day."

" In Arcady, if you go, you'll find the food is vile."

" What I look forward to most is the Cyclops Castle at Tiryns. We've a dwarf in our family, you see."

" There's nothing more lucky, is there? "

"Oh well, my dear, perhaps it may come, some day."

Clint turned.

" Come along, girls! "

" I shouldn't care to go with *them* on a walking tour. . . ."

" Mam'zelle Croizette, *chérie*, where ever have you been? "

" Looking for the Arbanel's bracelet."

" I'd forgotten it! ' The true-love-knot bangle he gave me when we became engaged.' "

Clint stood still.

"I don't know," she said, "but I believe I smell a rat."

"Fresh from the East, one is used to indelicate scents."

"Of course it's not for me to say. . . ."

"In a strange land, Miss Clint, we women should stand together."

"I noticed nothing until yesterday."

"And what did you notice then?"

"There's more than one trap set for Miss Collins."

"Lauk!"

"My gentleman's after her too."

"Oh, my poor strained nerves!"

"I suppose the bride's a bore."

"Of course she's neurasthenic and excitable and highly tuned. This morning, for instance, she sat and stormed at me because her white tennis shoes weren't white enough."

"Most young married women are ashamed of anything pale. . . . The Honourable Hester Dish on her wedding tour wore black all the time."

"Well, were there twenty traps laid for Miss Mabel she has too much gumption ever to go in."

"You astonish me! I'd have said now she would be very easily *épris*."

"Oh, mind the step!"

They had reached the Belvedere.

"I'd dearly like to carve my name on the leg of this seat."

"Without a fiancé's entwined, Miss Palmer, it looks almost as if——"

"*My* boy is in the Guards."

"Once I was engaged to a soldier."

"And you broke it off?"

"How he did bore me with his battles!"

Croizette peered down.

"Such a sunset," she remarked, "would have scared the ancients."

Palmer cleared her throat.

" I doubt it! . . ." she said. " When I went out into the world my dear mother told me a little about *them.* . . . There was the adventure of Titia Clarges. . . . She was one of those smart girls like the Midianites in Paris. Believe me, senility takes some scaring."

" Chatterbox! "

" What is the matter with Elizabeth? "

Elizabeth hid her face.

" There's a man," she said, " Miss Clint, carrying on in such a crazy way. . . . I think he means to draw us! "

" Let him ask permission."

" All this note-taking out of doors in my opinion really isn't nice. I'd as soon start hair-dressing in the street."

" It's on the cards you may. Professor Cowsend is to lecture in the Museum shortly from busts and coins and vases upon the Classic Coiffure. ' I shall expect you to attend,' Miss O'Brookomore said to me. ' It is never too l-l-late to learn! Campstools, flowers, unguents, pins and *peignoirs* provided. And we just sit down and do each other's hair."

" He'll not catch me there, I can promise him! "

" There'll be a prize."

" So I should hope! "

" The winner will have her expenses to any one of the islands—a day off."

" Who'd take an airing here from choice? "

" *Alone!* "

" Sprinkle ashes over me," Elizabeth murmured, " sooner! "

" Because Miss O'Brookomore's a bit of a bluestocking it doesn't signify that Dorinda, Lady Gaiheart's that way! Ours is quite another story. We're here to be nearer to Colonel Sweetish, who's at Malta. . . ."

" In your place, I'd not own it."

" How we do enjoy the saline breezes! ' Where's the wind? ' ' Which way's the wind? ' ' I don't know, your ladyship,' I reply, ' but it's as keen as mustard! ' "

Palmer examined her nails.

" My mistress isn't that sort," she said.

" What do you mean? "

" When I tapped at her door one night she didn't seem earthly. She came out to me with her pen in her hand, looking quite deranged—and old! My word! More like a mummy! "

" Worn out in intellectual excesses I dare say."

" *When she's with Miss Mabel she looks quite different.*"

" Were ever footsteps more out of tune! "

" An old dirge and a valse! "

Elizabeth giggled.

" Don't forget, Miss Palmer," she said, " you've promised to dance with me to-night when the band begins."

" Surely; only bear it, please, in mind, I never will dance gentleman."

" It doesn't matter. The chef said directly he'd finished he'd——"

" Finish me! "

" Whereabouts now were you born? "

" What makes you so inquisitive? "

" I could tell a London voice anywhere! Even in the dark."

" Hammersmith's my home."

" Hammersm——"

The Captive Women stared before them.

It was a bright and windy evening, with a mist that almost hid the sea. Now and then across Hymettos at a hint of sun swept a few pale shadows.

Miss Clint scanned the great groups of sailing clouds.

" Come along, girls," she murmured. " If it comes on to rain and we in our *derniers cris* . . .! "

XI

" NIGHT came with a big brown moon. . . . Ignatius knocked repeatedly on the door. At last a feeble voice —it was Haidèe's—cried: ' Come in! . . ' And I was led into the room by a Cowley Father. Oh, good gracious! "

" Go on. . . . His tired ecstasy makes me——"

" How's the poor head? "

" The dove did it good."

" I shouldn't have thought you had held it long enough."

" Quite long enough."

" Soon it'll grow weary of flying about the room."

" It sickens me so to watch it."

Miss Collins got up stealthily.

" Coo! "

" Don't, Mabel."

" It's looking at us both, dear, as much as to say . . ."

Miss O'Brookomore tittered.

" I believe all the time you're shamming."

" Oh, very well! "

" I'd do anything for you, Gerald."

" That's sweet. . . ."

" . . . It's exploring the ceiling now! "

" Open the window wide."

" Oh, listen! What tune is it? It's a slow-step of some sort."

The Biographer sat up slightly among her pillows.

" It sounds like the Incest-music," she murmured, " to some new opera."

" Oh, Gerald. . . . You do look bad. Upon my word you do."

" Really, Mabel, you have the tongue of a midwife, my dear."

" I'd run over to the pharmacy willingly if you thought. . . . It was they who invented the ' Eau de Parnasse.' It's made mostly out of sunflower seed. It's really *violets*."

" You'd stop to dance on the way! "

" Well? And if I did! "

" Just lately I've felt so nervous. I don't know why! "

" Accidents don't occur in a room full of people. Not often."

" It depends."

" Be good, Gerald. Now, there's a dear."

Miss O'Brookomore seemed touched.

" Run, twirl, dance, spin! " she said, " and come back in ten minutes."

" You're an angel."

" Carry me in your thoughts! "

" What good could *that* do you, Gerald? "

" Enjoy yourself—that's all."

In a black gauze gown with glorious garnitures, her hair tied up behind in a very Greek way, Miss Collins walked out into the hall where Miss Arne, to her surprise, was drilling a huge recruit.

" ' Good day, Lampito,' " she was saying, " ' dear friend from Lacedæmon. How well and handsome you look! What a rosy complexion! and how strong you seem; why, you could strangle a bull surely! ' "

The Australian girl grew rigid.

" ' Yes, indeed,' " she drawled, " ' I really think I could. 'Tis because I do gymnastics and practise the kick dance.' "

" There, of course, I think Lampito should throw up a leg. We'd better begin again."

Miss Collins paused.

" Haven't you got it pat by this time? " she inquired.

Miss Arne waved a fan with the names of some old
adorers scribbled across the sticks.

" Art," she remarked, " doesn't like being jostled.
How's your friend? "

" Gerald? She's pretty bad."

" Health is like a revue. It comes and goes. Even I
—in the morning when I rise I feel fit enough—at
least! . . . But by lunch-time I'm exhausted . . . and
then in the evening I'm myself again! . . ."

" Oh, good gracious! "

The Australian girl sat down.

" Phew! . . . It's warm acting! " she observed.

" We might have an ice."

" Won't you have a Vermouth-Cobbler with me? "

" What's that? "

" It's just a drink."

" Is it refreshing? "

" As a liqueur," Miss Collins said, " there's nothing
like *mint sauce*. You can't fancy what it's like alone."

The Colonial looked intriguing.

" Tell me about the stage," she implored, " or of
the people on your fan."

" I've forgotten! I forget! "

" Who's *Wellbridge?* "

" Ah! Dublin was a gay place when *he* was viceroy
there. . . ."

" Silent Stanley! "

" At the Garden Theatre he was Bassanio. . . ."

" Freddy Fortune?"

" Oh, my dear, he was the lover in Lady Twyford's
last play. He's the paramour in all her pieces."

" Alice."

Miss Arne took back her fan.

" I rang," she said to the waiter. " It's for an ice."

Miss Collins turned towards the ball-room. People either were pushing their way in or struggling to get out.

The Count touched her arm.

"Could you spare me half-an-ear for half-a-minute?" he asked.

"I'd sooner dance, if you don't mind."

"Are you fond of dancing?"

"I love it. Every winter nearly we give a ball. At least Mrs. Collins does. . . . It's really for me and Daisy. . . . We begin about half-past five and go on till about eight. After that there's a wizard."

"Outside the snow would be falling. The land would be white."

"Naturally *we* supply the rabbits."

"Have you much shooting?"

"We get all Lord Linco's birds as they fly across." The Count sighed.

"With us," he said, "it's mostly hares and larks."

"I suppose you mean the Opera."

"Indeed no!"

"Are you in the country much?"

"Now and then. My mother, you see, is obliged to be a good deal in Orvieto. She has also an apartment in Rome."

Miss Collins was mystified.

"*Apartments?*" she asked.

"An apartment, a flat, a floor—it is the first floor."

"Oh, good gracious!"

"This is your very first season, isn't it?"

"I don't know. I shouldn't care to say!"

"Excuse me."

"I live like a buried diamond half the year."

"Enjoy yourself now."

"Ah, that's . . . easier said than done . . ."

"Your friend ought not to be too hard on you."

"Gerald isn't really hard . . . You wouldn't say

56

so if you knew her well . . . Once she bought a little calf for some special binding, but let it grow up . . . and now it's a cow!"

They swung slowly out into the throng.

"I know this dance well. It's *Lady Randolph and the Old Shepherd!*"

"The old shepherd part is charming."

Miss Collins looked languid.

"Would you care to Cook me?" she asked.

"Cook you?"

"Show me round."

"Certainly. I should be delighted."

All Athens was responding to the dance. To Elizabeth, craning from the stairs, it seemed that the men resembled big black pearls while the women diamond drops—

"We might sit the rest out."

"Of course it's just as you like. . . ."

"There's such a moon!"

"I've just been reading to Gerald about the moon —a big brown one!"

"Do you read a lot?"

"Lately, out of pure politeness, I've been dipping into some of Gerald's spawn. But I never open a book unless I'm obliged. And my sister's just the same. Poor mite, she can't! . . . Oh, she's such a pickle! She is really *too* obstreperous. . . . You never know what she's up to!"

Mrs. Arbanel approached.

"What weapons can you muster," she asked, "besides darts?"

"Darts?"

"Did you bring a gun?"

"Gerald has a gold revolver. '*Honour*' she calls it."

"Well, to-morrow I and a few other women are going wild-duck shooting round Salamis, if you would care to come."

" Oh, wouldn't I enjoy it ! "

" We meet outside the church in the Rue d'Hermès at ten o'clock."

" Gerald is very particular about whom she meets."

" She can pick and choose. We're sure to be rather a band."

" I don't know what Gerald will say. . . ."

" I noticed there was a tray outside her door."

" We did all we could to tempt her. But she took her tea. And that was a mercy."

" It's nothing, I hope, serious ? "

" She gets these turns. . . . I think it's due to diet. Lately she has complained so much of her extraordin- arily vivid dreams. . . ."

Mrs. Arbanel smiled darkly.

" When I dream," she said, " I'm watching most."

" What—for instance ? "

" How do I know ? "

" Then don't expect me to say."

Mrs. Arbanel addressed the " Hippolytus Chario- teer " upon the ceiling.

" At the Rotunda," she murmured, as she moved away, " please to turn. . . ."

" What could she mean ? "

" I've not the least idea ! "

" Be careful of her if you go ! "

" She's a jealous fury. . . ."

" Her husband appears completely depressed."

" I fancy he wants me to dance."

" Don't ! And never let him."

" Why not ? "

" Little miss, when love springs under your nose ! . . ."

" Love ? . . ."

" Only dance with me ! "

" No. I'm going back to Gerald. Were anything to happen to her while I'm off duty I should never forgive myself."

Miss O'Brookomore had lowered her lights.

" Is that you, Mabel? " she asked.

" How's the poor head? "

" I've been drowsing."

" I'm glad you could manage that."

" Isn't the band *awful?* "

" Boom, boom, boom. . . ."

" Did you have a nice time? "

" I've found out one or two things by going down."

" What things? "

" Oh, Gerald, his mother keeps Apartments! "

" There. What did I tell you? "

" She has an Apartment in Rome. And I suppose it's a Boarding-house in the country. . . ."

" Well, to be sure! "

" After all, dear, Lady Frithelstock sells her fruit!"

" Even so! "

" And he has asked me, I think, to marry him."

" He's proposed? "

" Of course it's purely verbal . . ."

" What did he say? "

" First he asked to speak to me . . . and then he said, ' Little miss,' he said, ' when Love springs under your nose! . . .' That was his expression."

" A pretty one. But it has nothing to do with marriage. Oh, Mabel! "

" I long to be loved, Gerald."

" My dear."

" When he spoke of love it made me feel so important."

Miss O'Brookomore looked grim.

" You've yet to learn, I find, what frivolous things men are. . . ."

" What has that got to do with it, Gerald? "

" Be patient. You are sure to find a better *parti.*"

" A party? "

" A girl like you."

" And Mrs. Arbanel has invited us to join her at a shoot."

" In town? "

" At Salamis."

" It's so far off. . . ."

" Bring ' Honour,' she said."

" Honour's no use. It won't go off! "

" Oh, good gracious! "

" Besides, if I went I would lie on the Plage and watch you all."

" Gracious me, Gerald! "

" It's the dove again! "

" Unless I'm much mistaken, dear, that bird will stay in the room all night."

XII

A WARM, miraculous morning made the Athenian pavements split.

Before an Ikon in the little dark building of the Kapnikaræa Miss O'Brookomore knelt. And if she stopped long upon her knees most likely it was more that she found herself comfortable than anything else.

Miss Collins touched her arm.

" Oh, Gerald, we're all waiting for you," she said.

" I'm just coming."

" I shouldn't over care to be troubled by a conscience like that!"

The Biographer drew on a glove.

" After all," she inquired, " isn't heaven a sort of snobbism? A looking-up, a preference for the best hotel? "

" It's no good asking me, Gerald. It's like that button-hook of yours. . . ."

" We won't discuss that now."

" You don't imagine, do you, dear, I'd take your button-hook? I suppose you think I'd steal it!"

" Hush, Mabel!"

" I'm glad it isn't teaspoons. Although, of course, it's equally unpleasant."

Outside all was confusion, chatter, cracking of whips.

" *Βρεκεκεκέξ κοάξ κοάξ!* " Miss Arne harangued the mob.

" I don't suppose I shall knock down much," the Australian girl declared. " And, frankly, I don't much care. I'm one of those girls who wouldn't harm a fly. . . ."

" Dear Miss Dawkins. You'd think she was an auctioneer! "

With a sword-stick Mrs. Cowsend gave a sudden lunge into the air.

" In case the birds fly near," she said, " I shall simply prod them——"

" Mind the man."

" . . . δεν ἔχω χρήματα."

" What does he say? "

" He says he has no money."

" Hasn't he any? "

" οὐχί! "

" Apparently not. . . ."

" Oh, isn't it dreadful, Gerald? "

" Some of these heads are really rather fine."

" That looks like the English Consul! "

Miss Dawkins pressed her heart.

" Every time I see anyone——" she said.

" Is your father tall? "

" As we drive I shall give you all his measurements."

Along a sympathetic, winding road skirting the Acropolis their carriages made their way.

" All these open-air theatres amuse me," Miss Arne said. " It is like old *café-chantant* days."

Seated between Mrs. Arbanel and Dorinda, Lady Gaiheart, her personality struggled.

" Thank you, I never touch tobacco," Lady Dorinda said. " A cigarette with me would create a thirst. . . ."

" Fortunately Miss Dawkins has a flask."

" At the Antiquarians in Priam Place just now they've some nice Phœnician bottles."

Miss Collins nestled herself winningly against her neighbour.

" They showed me the smartest set of tea-things," she said, " that I ever saw. It belonged to Iphigenia —in Tauris. Oh, such little tiny cups! Such little teeny spoons! Such a darling of a cream-jug. . . . And such

a sturdy little tea-pot! With the sweetest spout. . . .
Pout. And a little sugar-basin! And a little slop-bowl.
. . ."

"I suppose all destined for America!"

Mrs. Arbanel turned and threw a few kisses to
someone in the brake behind.

"Who's the sun-helmet?"

"It's a Mrs. Lily Gordon Lawson—she has that
big new villa on the Olympian Road. You know."

"They say Olympia for Love!"

"For love?"

"If people should come together there—it's all
up with them."

"My dear, to see Greece, it's what I came out
for!"

"Well, somewhere in me, far down," Miss Dawkins
declared, "I don't mind admitting, there's a field
with cows browsing."

"Have you been seeking them long?"

"Almost always."

"Just wandering!"

"Hotels, always hotels. *Yes!* And one does get
so tired of tavern life!"

"You must be very weary."

"After this I propose to do the I's . . . India,
Italy, Ireland, Iceland. . . ."

"When you've found them you'll be so bored."

Miss Dawkins raised to her lips her flask.

"What ever is in it?" Miss Collins asked.

Miss Dawkins fixed her.

"It's a digestive—cocktail," she said at last. "Or
a *Blue Brazilian*, as some people prefer to call it . . .
that is so."

Mrs. Arbanel gave a cry.

"The *sea*."

"Have you never seen it?"

"Mabel! . . ."

" What emerald or sapphire! " Miss Arne asked. " Aren't you ravished? "

" I mean to bathe," Miss Collins announced.

" My dear, how can you ? "

" Oh, Gerald, just a dip! "

Dorinda, Lady Gaiheart, relaxed.

" Colonel Sweetish and Captain Muckmaisie, both old and very dear friends of mine," her attitude seemed to say, " are somewhere across that light. . . ."

" How many guns are there? "

" Not so many as there seem. Neither Mrs. Cowsend nor Lady Dorinda will be shots. They're only going to pick up the birds."

Mrs. Cowsend chuckled.

" Like good retrievers," she said.

Mrs. Arbanel turned to throw an extra kiss.

" There's Mrs. Erso-Ennis and Mrs. Viviott," she said.

" Those two! "

" And little Mrs. Lawson, who's really *très sport*. . . ."

" She says she's sure she shall shoot someone! "

" Oh, she's clever, she's fascinating."

Miss Collins scowled.

" I should like her to start trying her tricks on me!"

" And then there're ourselves."

" I've no gun," Miss O'Brookomore said. " At most I could throw a book. . . ."

" What have you brought with you? "

" I've my Wordsworth."

" Is he your poet? "

" I'm told I should read *Le Charme d'Athènes*," Mrs. Cowsend said. " But I always disliked that series."

" I fancy there's a new one: *Notes on the Tedium of Places*—comprising almost everywhere."

Miss Collins glanced at her guardian.

64

"It's extraordinary Gerald doesn't go dotty," she observed, "writing as she does. . . ."

"Does the *Life* progress?"

"It's enough to say it assumes proportions."

Lady Dorinda spread out her parasol.

"The Kettler cult seems the only shade we have to speak of!" she said. "Since . . . Eleusis."

Mrs. Cowsend freckled faintly.

"Were I to have a baby girl here," she said at random, "O'Brien would insist on calling her Athene; and it would be Olympia. Or Delphine. Or, if on the way there, Helen! . . ."

"I should have thought Violet, or *Violets*," Mrs. Arbanel suggested as the carriage stopped.

Across a vivid, a perfectly pirate sea, Salamis showed shimmering in the sun.

Miss Arne held out arms towards it.

"It's like a happy ending!" she breathed.

Boats were in readiness.

"Where's the wind?" the Countess sniffed.

"There's almost an autumnal feel, isn't there?"

The wild apple-trees along the shore stood tipped with gold.

"Perhaps we shall see Pan!"

Mrs. Arbanel shouldered her gun.

"To avoid accidents," she said, "we should drift about in line."

"My dear, I always fire sideways!"

Mrs. Viviott covered up her ears.

"Don't!" she said.

"Why not?"

"I never could bear the crack-of-a-gun business," she confessed.

"Then what ever made you come?" Miss Collins queried.

"Mainly for Mrs. Erso-Ennis—to look after her."

" ' And the sun went down and the stars came out far over the summer sea! '—eh, Gerald? "

Miss O'Brookomore looked blank.

" I hope you know we're sweeping straight south-west! " she murmured presently. . . ." I've an ink-ling there's Megara."

" It was above Megara the Seymoures——"

Overhead the sky was purely blue.

Miss Arne scanned it.

" What is that large bird? " she inquired.

" Where? "

Miss Dawkins picked up an imaginary guitar.

> " ' That which yonder flies,' " [she sang]
> " ' Wild goose is it?—Swan is it?
> Wild goose if it be—
>> Haréya tōtō,
>> Haréya tōtō,
> Wild goose if it be,
> It's name I soon shall say. . . .
> Wild swan if it be—better still!
>> Tōtō! ' "

" Enchanting! "

" I learnt it in Japan—that is so."

Miss Collins drooped.

" The water's so clear you can see everything that's going on."

" Couldn't we moor ourselves somewhere and anchor? "

" I could fancy I hear turtle doves," Lady Dorinda remarked.

" Oh, they're city! "

Miss Arne appeared to pray.

" I love Finsbury Circus for its Doves," she said.

" And I adore the Aspens in Cadogan Square. . . ."

" Does the sea upset you? "

" Oh, Gerald! . . . She's certainly going to be queer."

" I'm fond of that garden too, behind Farm Street, with those bow-windows staring out upon it. I could sit for ever huddled up in a black frock there exciting sympathy . . . listening to the priests' voices in the Farm."

Miss Collins jumped up.

" Don't, Mabel! You'll capsize the boat."

Mrs. Cowsend shuddered.

" I never could swim," she said.

" I trust the gods would drop down strings—a sort of parachute affair—drawing us through the water."

Mrs. Viviott addressed her friend.

" Were yours to give, Geneviève! . . ." she said.

" That's just *you*, Iris! "

Miss O'Brookomore fluttered her eyelids.

" Did you ever see such a rag of a sail? "

" It's black."

" O-h, there went a fish with wings! "

" With——"

" Where? "

" Oh, my dear——! "

Mrs. Arbanel turned her gun about and—fired.

XIII

" I SHALL never forget the hideous moment! "

" They're driving her round the town."

Lady Dorinda slowly wiped an eye.

" To the departed," she said, " short cuts are dis-respectful."

" I know Athens pretty well," Mrs. Viviott de-clared. " And they're going a statesman's way! "

Miss Collins threw herself into an easy seat.

" Oh, it's awful, awful, awful! " she said. " It doesn't do to think. . . ."

The Room of the Minerva in the National Museum lay steeped in light.

" It's as though one held a Memorial service to her somehow," Miss O'Brookomore commented, " amidst all these busts and urns and friezes. . . ."

" For the Lysistrata that Nymph in the corner was to have inspired her gown. ' I shall play her in lavender and helio,' she said to me. And now, poor dear, where is she? "

" Oh, it's awful, it's hideous!" Miss Collins broke out . . . " To-day I feel turned forty! This has made an old woman of me. Oh, good gracious! "

In her silver hat crowned with black Scotch roses drawn down close across the eyes she might perhaps have been taken for more.

" Mr. Arbanel, poor man, seems almost to be broken. Vina's vulgar violence, he said, disgusts me more than I can ever say—and when her maid went to her door she said, ' Go away! I'm Proser-pine.' "

" Oh. . . . If anyone had *told* me, Gerald, that I'd

68

become acquainted with a bride-murderess . . . I should never have believed it."

" What do they intend to do? "

" Decamp—if they're wise."

" When I saw her in her black dress, Gerald! "

" It was a pure accident—naturally, she said, when questioned."

" One tries to believe it was."

" She *would* wave her gun about so. I was in terrors all the time! "

" I suppose there was an inquest? " Miss Collins said.

" I really couldn't say. . . ."

" I should like to have been at it."

" One longs for the country now—to get away."

" We leave for Delphi directly," Miss O'Brookomore said.

" Kettling? "

" Well . . . more or less. . . . Poor Kitty, she went to Delphi to consult the Oracle and found it had gone. You can imagine her bitterness."

" I dare say she consoled herself with the fruit. . . . There's a garden on the way to Itea. . . . You never *saw* such apples! "

" I dare say that's gone too."

" Be careful in Olympia."

" What *does* one do in Olympia? Tell me, please! " Mrs. Viviott fetched a sigh.

" Oh, well," she said, " of course one sits, and sits, and sits, and *sits*, before the Praxiteles. . . . And then, if two people come together there I warn you they're sure to fall in love. . . ."

Miss O'Brookomore bowed.

" Here're more mourners! " she exclaimed.

" Oh, isn't it gruesome, Gerald? "

" We turned in here, dear," Mrs. Cowsend said. " I didn't feel I wanted to go on. . . ."

" That turquoise tinsel thing—*violet*, I should say —the pall! "

The Historian seemed to touch it.

" It was her doom, poor dear. . . . On the voyage out I've a recollection still of the way she sat on board while the waves burst over her."

" At any rate she had the sad satisfaction of dying in Greece."

" My dear, there was no time for reflections! "

Miss Collins covered her face.

" Was there no post-mortem? " she inquired.

Mrs. Cowsend showed distress.

" Have you been to look at the coiffures yet? " she asked. " It's to-day my husband holds his classes, and they're all in the Vase Room now."

" There's a room set aside somewhere for the ' Obscene,' " Miss Collins said. " Where is it? "

" My dear, how could one think of such a thing at such a minute!"

" Only to distract us."

" The Professor's classes are more likely to do that."

" In Arcadia," Miss O'Brookomore declared, " I intend to coil my hair like rams' horns."

Mrs. Viviott vibrated.

" My dear," she said, " I never vary. I *couldn't!* "

" In Arcadia you'll find the continual singing of the cicadas require some excluding."

Lady Dorinda raised a hand.

" Were I the wife of a gunner," she protested, " it would make no difference. I should always be high! "

Miss Collins slipped an arm about her companion's waist.

" Oh . . It's a Dance of the Hours, Gerald! "

" Dance of the Drumerdairies, my dear."

" Whose doing was it? "

Miss O'Brookomore appeared absorbed. . . . For

a moment Time hovered, wobbled, swerved. Miss Collins aged for her.

"It's lovely, Mabel," she said, "when—— Oh, Mabel!" she said.

Miss Collins started.

"This caps everything!" she exclaimed.

"Is there anything wrong, dear?"

"Mrs. Arbanel's actually dressing. . . ."

Mrs. Viviott glided forward.

"Geneviève!" she implored—"Geneviève *Erso-En-n-is!*"

Miss Collins caught at the Historian.

"Let us go, Gerald," she said, "before it happens again."

XIV

" It's nice to be in Delphi, Gerald! "

" After Athens," Miss O'Brookomore said, " it really is delightful."

" . . . We never saw the king and queen, dear."

" No more we did! "

" This morning I followed an empty river bed for miles and miles. . . ."

" To do justice to the walks," Miss O'Brookomore observed, " one would need to have legs as hard, pink and resisting as a ballerina."

" Aren't you going round to look at the Auriga as usual? "

" I hardly know. Possibly I may take a turn presently in the direction of Parnassos. . . ."

" There's a shrub in the garden, Gerald, all covered in mauve rosettes! "

" It's perhaps a Delphinium."

" Oh! I do think it sweet! "

" I wonder who's here beside ourselves."

" I noticed the names of Cyril Cloudcap and of Charlie Cumston in the Visitors' Book. . . ."

" That sounds English."

" They left yesterday for Olympia, and there was a Mrs. Clacton, Gerald."

" Has she gone too? "

" The Count said we weren't to be surprised if——"

" My dear, if Pastorelli turns up here we move on."

" Fussy, fidgety thing! "

" When he makes that sort of *clearing* noise . . . No! Really——"

" That's nothing, Gerald. Why I do it myself."

Miss O'Brookomore stared hard at the floor.

" I miss a carpet," she said.

" In my bedroom at home, Gerald, the carpet has big blue tulips on a yellow ground."

" Has the postman been? "

" He's been."

" Wasn't there anything? "

" There was a letter from mum. And another from Daisy."

" I thought she couldn't write."

" She sets her mark."

" Let me see."

" It's only a smear."

" Is the house disposed of—does your mother say? "

" I conclude it isn't. She says the greenfly this year has destroyed almost everything. Hardly anybody has been spared. At Patchpole Park the peaches just dried on the walls as though they were dates. And she's quite in despair about Daisy! She says she gets more hopeless hourly. She's taking her into York so as to have her ears pierced, poor mite. And papa, he's at Helstan with Napier—it's that new seaside——"

" Is the Count aware you're fidanzata? "

" I didn't tell him I wasn't quite free, and I don't think I will. I must write to Napier, I suppose, and break it off—I feel sorry for him, poor boy."

Miss O'Brookomore wandered to the window.

" It's going to be hot to-day."

" In the Gulf there's been rain in two places."

" Here we've the sun."

" What ever would the vines do, Gerald, without the olives to hold them up? "

" I can't think."

" They always say at home nothing can compare with the view from Mockbird Hill. On a clear day you can see to Ditchley."

73

Miss O'Brookomore shaded her eyes.

" There's an arrival," she said.

" Oh! "

" What is it? "

" He's here! "

" Oh! Mabel! "

" Oh! Gerald! "

" Oh! Mabel! "

" Oh! Gerald! "

Hand meeting hand, palm meeting palm (the vitality of the one rambling off into the other), they sought to find vent to their emotion.

XV

THE inn of the Pythian Apollo winked its lights.

Moving about the bare boards of her room, Miss O'Brookomore made her box. Now bending, now rising, now falling to her knees, it appeared from the road below as though she were imploring for forgiveness.

> " For I am the old King's daughter,
> The *youngest*, sir, said she!
> The King he is my father,
> And my name is Marjorie. . . .
>
> Oh, my name is Marjorie, she said,
> My father he is the King,
> I am the youngest child he had,
> And what will to-morrow bring?
>
> What will to-morrow bring, she said,
> Oh, what will to-morrow bring?
> The King he is my father,
> And what will to-morrow bring? "

" . . . Gerald, she always sings as she packs! Just making it up as she goes——"

" Why is she in such a hurry to be off? "

" I don't know. To-day she's been all veins and moods, whims and foibles."

" Induce her to remain."

" If only she would. . . . We haven't yet been up to the Cave of the Nymphs! "

" Ecco! "

" It's annoying to have to miss it."

75

"One night I sat upon the stairs
And heard him call my name!
I crept into the darkness
And covered my head for shame.

I covered my head for shame, she said,
Oh, I covered my head for shame!
The King he is my father,
And I covered my head for shame."

"Sometimes when she starts to sing she'll keep it up for hours. It depends on what she's doing!"

"My sister Yoland she is dead,
And Ygrind is no more. . . .
They went away to Ireland,
And nobody knows where they are!

Nobody knows where they are at all,
No one seems able to say——"

"Will you come for a little stroll?"
"Where ever to?"
"Anywhere."
She raised her eyes towards Parnassos, whose cold white heights glimmered amid the stars.
"Oh, it gets grimmish!"
"You shouldn't be afraid."
"Tell me," she asked, "would it be a Pension?"
"A Pension?"
"Those apartments of your mother's."
"What does it matter now?"
"Oh! . . . Perhaps I ought to aid poor Gerald!"
"Aiding harms the hands."
"Mine are spoilt already."
"I can't believe it."
"Mum pretends my hands are large because Time hangs heavy upon them."

" Time in the country, they say, is apt to drag."

" Not if there's a farm. Who could be bored by watching the manners of some old surly bull, or a dog on the scent of things, or a dove paying visits? "

" Very likely! "

" You're blasé."

" Nothing of the sort."

" Poor little Geraldine, her weariness exceeds most things. She says the world's an ' 8.' "

" That's better than an ' o.' "

" The repetition palls."

" There is always a nuance."

" It's better to be an Indifferentist, she says. Not to care! But if anything ever goes wrong . . . It's impossible not to smile at her philosophy."

" You must be her comfort."

" I don't know what she'd do without me. Because the maid's a perfect fool. When we arrive anywhere usually it's I who improve the terms. . . . Gerald hates to bargain. She seems to think it sordid. So I do it for her. Oh, it's such fun! . . . Is it to be a back room or a front room, with a double bed or a single bed, or would the lady disdain a back bedroom without any balcony? Then Gerald asserts herself. ' The lady requires a balcony with an unobstructed horizon ' —and if there isn't such a thing, then we try elsewhere."

He stooped a little.

" It's the case of a courier," he said.

" I think we ought to turn."

" We will," he answered, " when the road bends. Remember, the world's an ' 8 '! "

XVI

"WILL you talk to me about the Moon and Stars? . . .
Would it amuse you?"

Miss O'Brookomore raised herself. . . . A young
man whom she had never seen until now stood before
her.

"I shall be delighted to talk to you about anything,"
she replied.

"When did you arrive?"

"My dear, we only got here yesterday."

There came a voice of protest.

"Oh, Gerald! It was the day before."

"What are your impressions of Olympia?"

"I love it, I think it sweet."

"Everybody says the same."

Miss OBrookomore breathed a sigh.

"I should like you to be my Literary Executor,"
she said.

He knelt down and took her hand.

"No, my dear Thing!" he answered. "I'm sorry
—but I simply can't. Simply I should love to, my dear
Thing! But it's impossible. . . ."

Miss Collins rose discreetly.

"Gerald—I think I shall leave you," she said.

XVII

" Who ever was it, Gerald? . . ."

Seated before a mirror, her shoulders gilded by the evening sun, Miss O'Brookomore drew a net of sapphire stones across her hair.

" Some god of the woods—no doubt! "

" That's only for a diary. . . . It doesn't do for me. . . ."

" Things do happen so quickly! "

" Very likely it was Cyril Cloudcap. . . ."

" It may have been Charlie Cumston."

" Mer-cy! Gerald."

" How soon will you be ready? "

" I've no appetite, Gerald. While the Count's at Delphi I don't seem to care."

" Foolish girl! "

" Oh! I do long to be married, Gerald. . . . It's what I long to be most. Just married, dear."

" Not without your parents' consent."

" Nonsense, Gerald! "

" It's a caprice that will pass."

" Oh, Gerald, his love talk with me and what I reply—it's a real duet! "

Miss O'Brookomore tucked a few mauve satin flowers into her frock.

" Aren't they heavenly? " she inquired. " Especially the purple ones. . . ."

" Oh, Gerald! "

" My poor puss——"

" People's lives, dearie, don't seem to be a bit their own once they're in love."

" Love is a seed that needs watering from day to day. Otherwise it dies."

" With me it all accumulates."

" Don't let's miss the sunset—the later half."

" It's a sunset and a sobset, Gerald. Oh, it's so sad. . . ."

" In the end everything has to be paid for."

" Principally for that I'd sooner I didn't dine. It really isn't worth it, Gerald. . . ."

" No dinner? "

" Even gratis. Oh, Gerald! "

" We're sure to meet the Arbanels."

" I tapped at their door as I came along."

" I fear that was intrusive."

" Directly it dawned upon her it was me she flew forward brandishing a powder-puff."

" Her behaviour's getting Byzantine—more and more."

Miss Collins folded an arm about her friend.

" Why do you think it's Byzantine, Gerald? What ever makes you think it is? "

" On certain natures environment frequently reacts. I can recall the Queen of Snowland (when a guest at Windsor) frisking off one afternoon into the town in search of lodgings. She came to the very house where I was writing her life . . . and we met in the front hall."

" Oh, good gracious! "

" Similarly, I feel inclined to believe that Mrs. Arbanel in Egypt would be less vivid and more *Athenian* in her ways."

" Can a leopard change its spots, Gerald? "

" My dear, it can modify them."

" I'm surprised you lend her Palmer."

" I've only offered her, of course, until the faithless Clint can be replaced. Mrs. Arbanel hopes to secure someone locally."

" I shouldn't think there were many maids to be found locally, Gerald. I shouldn't think there was one. Not in Olympia."

" The deciphering of their characters, in any case, would require a skilful student," Miss O'Brookomore observed as Palmer came in.

Miss Collins rolled her eyes.

" Thank heaven! " she exclaimed.

" It didn't take you long! "

" I was as quick with her, miss, as I could be."

" We were prepared to hear some screams. . . ."

" Were I to be stabbed, Miss Mabel, I should endeavour to be considerate."

" Violets! "

" I suppose, poor thing, she is still very dazed? "

" She seemed lost in reverie, miss."

" I expect it's the air."

" She intends to ride to Sparta almost immediately, since Olympia, she hears, is nothing but cliques and coteries."

" It's their season now."

" There's a good deal of entertaining, miss, to-night. Dorinda, Lady Gaiheart, is to have a party for the Irish Archæological School. And Mrs. L. G. Lawson is bringing over some of her friends from the Villa Sophonisba."

Miss O'Brookomore began muffling a foot up in a silver-spangled shoe.

" Had I been told earlier I'd have gone into Corinth," she said.

" No doubt you'd have found Miss Dawkins there."

" My dear, she's in Olympia. She arrived this afternoon. I overheard her telling her father's chest-measurements to the boy that works the lift."

" And I dare say half-seas-over? "

" Poor thing."

" Oh, she's so common, Gerald! "

" I should like to be on a balcony, miss, for the Recognition."

" I dare say she'll be made to display her birthmarks first."

" There's no need, miss—if you'll pardon me—for birthmarks with a face like that."

" Brute! . . . You've pricked me. . . ."

The sound of the dinner-gong came dwindling up.

" Oh, the way they beat it! "

Miss O'Brookomore smothered a sigh.

" It might be the Ramadan! " she declared.

XVIII

O stars! O perfumes! O night!

In the grey cedar crests, from the blue fir-trees of the Kronian hill, the owls flapped gabbling; among the fields of mournful olives the cicadas called; over the fragments of fallen marble, crushing the wild thyme, the fire-flies flashed; and on the verandah of the Hôtel de France, the scintillation of her diamonds harmonising equally with the heavens as with the earth, Dorinda, Lady Gaiheart was finishing a tale.

"He then walked off with her," she said, "in an appalling pair of old black slippers."

"He didn't run!"

"Why should he? Men seldom run away with girls. Not in these days."

Miss O'Brookomore looked relieved.

"I always think of Europa," she said.

"That comes from chattering so much about farms."

"With daughters of your own I was determined to consult you."

"I never bothered. They were just a nest of sisters, until one by one, alas, without requiring my advice, they deserted the family tree."

> "Her hour of love,
> How soon it passed!
> It passed ere Mary knew.

And that is the worst of all these rash marriages."

"I fear the Arbanels are already getting fidgety."

"She was crying so much at dinner, poor thing."

"He was telling me they propose to plant a bed of

83

violets, big white single ones, on the Acropolis, to the glory of the delicate and individual artiste, *Arne* —the 'only' Lady Teazle of our time—in the presence of the *corps diplomatique* and the king and queen."

" Tears! "

" Toilettes! "

" Speeches! "

" I expect so! "

Miss Dawkins dropped a sigh.

" Where's Troy? " she said, wheeling round in her chair.

" You surely don't think they're there! "

Lady Dorinda looked reserved.

" I must rejoin my friends," she murmured. " In a few minutes we're all going over to the ruins."

Miss O'Brookomore lifted up her eyes.

" I shall stay where I am for the new girl dancer," she devoutly mumbled.

" Is she one of the Sophonisba set? "

" Mrs. Viviott found her . . . whirling to herself among the Treasuries."

" At Tanagra," Miss Dawkins said, " she was balancing herself, not long ago, in the village street. I was obliged to interrupt her to ask if a smart fair woman with an elderly, stoutish man had been seen that way: S-s-s-s-h! she said. In the evening when the peacocks dance . . ."

" I should be afraid of her! "

" She is really wildly pretty."

" Those deep wonder-rings about her eyes are quite unholy."

" At dinner Mrs. Viviott sat like a player with an unsatisfactory hand at cards."

" I hate all ingratitude," Miss O'Brookomore observed. " In Biography, of course, one sees so much of it. . . ."

" Tell me! How is *it* getting on? "

" Gaps! Gaps! ! Gaps! ! ! "

" There are bound to be a few."

" Did you ever meet Max Metal? " Miss Dawkins asked.

" No, never."

" Or Nodo Vostry? "

" I don't remember him."

" Or Harry Strai? "

" I'm sure I never did! "

" Why? . . ."

" In my opinion their books for girls are full of unsound advice."

" I'm glad I can still sometimes drug my senses with a book," Lady Dorinda exclaimed.

" Unluckily, racing round as I do, I very rarely find a chance."

" You must have met with some adventures by the way."

Miss Dawkins mixed herself a sombre liqueur.

" I had a good time in Smyrna," she drowsily declared.

" Only there? "

" Oh, my dears, I'm weary of streets; so weary! "

" And have you never found any trace——? "

" At Palermo, once. . . . I was wandering in the Public Gardens before the hotel, amid blown bus tickets and autumn leaves, when I thought I saw them. Father, anyway. He was standing at an open window of an eau-de-Nil greenhouse. He looked very much younger—altered almost to be a boy. I stood and stared. He smiled. I believe I spoke. And then, before I was able to realise it, I was inside his dark front hall. . . ."

" Who was he? "

" I can only tell you he was a dear thing. I shall hope to meet him in heaven."

Mrs. Arbanel swooped up lightly.

" I respond to the sound of the sea," she said, " and the tinkle of ice! "

" Let me make you a Cherry Cobbler."

" After interviewing a temporary-maid there's nothing I'd like *more!* "

" Are you satisfied? "

" Is one ever——"

" Still, if she understands hair! "

" That is all she seemed to follow."

" She'll do, I'm sure, for Sparta."

Miss O'Brookomore unfurled her fan.

" Frankly, I rather shrink from Sparta," she said.

" What is there to take one there? "

" I really forget—I believe there's a crouching Venus."

" What does Mr. Arbanel say? "

" He doesn't say anything. He leaves me to go alone."

" What? Isn't he going at all? "

" When the weather is milder he may."

" A man will have his comforts," Lady Dorinda affirmed.

" I long to hear about your new home."

" . . . Oh well. . . . It's quite a clever little house. . . . Five bedrooms. . . ."

" Modest."

" If you would care to see the plans——"

" My dear, there's no hurry," Miss Dawkins said. " Any-old-time will do."

Miss O'Brookomore turned her head stiffly towards the stars.

On all sides through the dusk, intermingling with faint nocturnal noises, rose up a sound of kisses.

She shivered as she felt something touch her own exceedingly sensitive skin.

" Where have you been, Mabel? " she asked.

86

" Writing letters. I've been describing the Temples to mum."

" Writing letters," Mrs. Arbanel said. " I think it must be an Olympic Game."

" Why, what? "

" Do you ask me for the rules? "

" How should I know—the rules? "

" They're really very simple. . . . You sit two at a table. A young man, perhaps, and a chit of a girl. With a piece of plate-glass in between. And then, when you've drummed with your fingers and played with your pen, you shuffle with your feet, and you throw dying glances over the top."

Miss Collins challenged.

" . . . Prove it! " she said.

" Wild girl! You surely don't suppose I'm going to prove it? "

" Why, I was sitting with a widow! "

Miss Dawkins speared herself a cherry.

" Oh, for a quiet corner! "

" First, Mrs. Lawson's guest is going to dance."

" Who, exactly, is she? "

" She's a pupil of Tasajara, Gerald."

Miss O'Brookomore's nose grew long.

" I never heard of her," she said.

" Oh, she's a study, Gerald."

" One sees so many artists here——"

" With a water-colour in the Academy. Some people seem to think it permissible to look a little mad and to behave as if they *really* were. . . ."

" I heard the flowers scream as I picked them! " Mrs. Erso-Ennis was saying as she scattered a shower of blossoms upon the floor.

" If it's to be Botticelli——" Miss O'Brookomore complained.

Mrs. Erso-Ennis looked indignant.

"Botticelli! . . . I invented the whole thing just now."

87

" How could you! "

" It's the *Hesitation of Klytemneſtra*. The poor Queen, you see, cannot quite bring herself to kill the King, and while he sleeps she performs a suite of intereſting, *idyllic* poses over him with a knife."

" Better wait, Gerald," Miss Collins advised.

Mrs. Erso-Ennis flung a few laſt leaves of roses.

" Oh! Think of the earwigs! "

" In these old-fashioned places one should only wear short skirts."

" At the summer sales in Athens," Miss Dawkins seraphically said, " I picked up a regular siren's gown. . . . Looped up upon one side to reveal the knee."

" What you have now, if one may say so, is also very original."

" It doesn't fit. But it isn't meant to," Miss Dawkins replied.

Mrs. Erso-Ennis direĉted her eyes to the room.

On a couch, deſtined to be the royal bed, a young woman, evidently a prima donna, was caressing rapturously her little boy.

" My son," she was saying, " my opera . . . x! Opera . . . xx ! My Johannes . . . !! My *bébé!* . . ."

" She muſt be removed, I fear."

" And there're some horrid arrivals, too."

For those with ears fine enough Miss Collins caused an innocent bud to wail.

" Oh, Gerald," she said, " who do you think is here? "

" Not——! "

" He's in the bus, dearie! "

" My poor puss . . . You've turned quite pale."

" Oh, the shock to me, Gerald! . . ."

" You look so tired, dear . . . so sad and so worn out."

" It's because I'm dead beat, Gerald."

" Feel faint, at all ? "

" No—but I've never felt like this before, Gerald.
. . . You little know how I feel—I could not have
believed it was possible."

XIX

" Sixteen of them," she counted, " and a diamond drop!"

"*Au revoir*. Until to-night."

" Oh, the rush!"

" You're ready? Packed——"

" All I dare. I could hardly bring away my big box —the one with the furs and flannels! . . ."

" You'll need your passport."

" It's lost."

" Lost!"

" Gerald must have burnt it, she says, among her papers. She's everlastingly burning things. She lights her fire in the evening just as she bolts her door. . . . And then she burns things, and dreams things, and pokes things, and mutters things—*l'heure exquise*, she calls it."

" . . . Very likely."

" I've an idea it's rheumatics, poor soul. . . ."

" M-a-b-e-l!" Miss O'Brookomore called again.

" I must go to her. . . ."

" One kiss!"

" O-o-o-o-h!"

" Another!"

" Not till we get in the train."

" *Cara mia dolce!*"

" And thanks very much for the diamonds," Miss Collins replied.

Loitering up and down the hall among the tubs of orange-trees—now in full flower—Miss O'Brookomore was growing ruffled.

" It's charming!" she said. " It appears he's on our floor."

" Oh no, he's not, Gerald . . . He's on the floor above. Right overhead, dearie."

Miss O'Brookomore looked away.

" There are people, I find, who have no heads," she ruefully remarked. " They've lost them."

" I don't know why you should dislike him, Gerald. Because he doesn't you. He calls you the pretty priestess. . . ."

The Biographer unbent a shade.

" Does he? " she inquired.

" Are you going for your walk? "

" I told Miss Dawkins we would help her to find her parents."

" It's too late to go far, dearie."

" Nonsense! "

" How can she expect to find them, Gerald, sitting all day with a Gin Daisy or a Brandy Flip? Tell me that now! "

" Anyway we might take a turn round the garden. . . . If they're here at all I expect they're in the shrubbery."

It was the hour when, to a subtle string band, the bustling waiters would be bringing tea.

" Oh, the Sophonisbas, Gerald!—some of them."

Their tired, art-stained faces turned towards a little Saint with rose lips, eyes and crown, Mrs. Erso-Ennis and Mrs. Viviott were overwhelming with attentions the pupil of Tasajara.

" Mercy, Gerald! "

" Hein! "

" There's bound to be heart-burnings, Gerald."

" . . . I shouldn't wonder."

" And there's your God-of-the-Wood, dearie. . . ."

Miss O'Brookomore changed her course.

" Not before the windows! " she exclaimed.

" Olympia for love, Gerald."

" Olympia for tattle."

" Oh, Gerald! I mean to fling in my lot with a crowd of absolute strangers. . . ."

" What! "

" Love isn't logical, Gerald."

" Alas! "

" Oh! Gerald! "

" What has your friend a year? "

" How should I know, dearie? "

" It's important to know."

" It's better to be poor—I've often heard mum say—than to have a soft seat in hell."

" An Italian is very easily enamoured."

" I love his dark plastered hair, Gerald. I think it quite sweet."

" It isn't enough. . . ."

" He's like somebody from Marathon, Gerald! "

" You're young yet."

" Oh, Gerald, when he sang the Shepherd-Star-Song from *Tannhäuser* and gave that shake! . . . You can't think how much I was moved . . . How I responded. . . ."

" His *catches from Butterfly* would get on my nerves!"

" Had I nerves like you I couldn't rest without a passport."

" It's tiresome, I admit."

" It's that, dearie. . . ."

" Don't despond! "

" Suppose they detained you, Gerald? "

" Why, we'd sing a duet together."

" Wait till there's a warrant! "

" A warrant? "

" Sometimes I think of the prison we saw in Patras, with the prisoners all thrusting their heads out between the bars."

" Don't, Mabel! "

" Oh, Gerald! It's a climax and a perfect semax, dear."

" We're not helping Miss Dawkins at all! "

" You go one way, Gerald. And I'll go another. . . ."
Miss O'Brookomore glanced behind her.

Already the sun-topped hills were lost in lilac towards the ground. It would soon be night.

" Very well," she murmured, letting fall a glove; " we will meet again at dinner."

XX

" MABEL! Mabel! Mabel! Mabel!
Mabel! Mabel! Mabel! Mabel! "

XXI

HOTEL CENTRAL,
CONSTITUTIONAL PLACE,
ATHENS.

Saturday.

DEAR GERALD,—I was married this morning and we
leave to-morrow early for Corfu don't worry about
me dear I'm alright O darling I'm the happiest girl in
Greece I wore my little amber tricorne satin cap dear
and Oio gave me the violets I shall get my trousseau
bit by bit I suppose as we go along I had wanted rather
badly to be married in the Kapnikaraea but it was a
Registry after all good-bye now Gerald and take care
of yourself dear do in haste yrs always affectionately
MABINA PASTORELLI.

P.S.—I laughed the whole time the priest who
married us would keep whisking his skirt.

Mrs. Cowsend is here still Old ox.

Oio says if I write another word he'll pour all my
ink away.

PART II

" Do you remember that picture of Jesus that poor Miss Turner used to show us?" The Honey-suckle—D'ANNUNZIO

I

THE sunlight passing through the glass candlestick by the bedside shot out its rays towards her threefold and woke her with a start.

—Bovon! Home!

—The Countess gaped.

There was the fine old carpet stained with tulips, and the familiar text upon the lightly figured walls, and the dress bust in the corner behind the *causeuse* that cast its consoling outline so effectively at night, and the medicine chest above the rocking-chair, with the sage-chinoiseries on top, that would swing their heads in the affirmative almost for a glance—which responsiveness had been known to work like a spell upon certain sensitive natures in more instances than one.

The Countess sat up.

" Bianca! " she called.

By the wide " Elysium " bed stood a bassinet tricked in bows.

" Bianca, Borghese, Nancy, Sabina! "

From the doorway came a whirl of skirts—a croon—and Mrs. Collins entered.

" While the mother was asleep the granny came and stole the darling, and whipped down the corridor, out into the garden, and round and round the house."

The Countess held out her arms.

" Oh, my honey bear! "

" Don't, Mabel. You'll kill it."

" Oh, the interesting little pickle! Oh, the Roman rascal! . . . Poveretta! *Ah, Dio!* "

Mrs. Collins considered her daughter.

" . . . There's something I want to say to you," she said.

" Yes, what is it? "

" Everyone's inquiring for the Count—all the Bovon busybodies."

" Kra, kra, Mrs. Rook."

" They're concerned he hasn't come! "

" It's the Vintage. Directly that's over he will."

Mrs. Collins beamed affectionately.

" In any case," she murmured, " I mean to give a small dinner for you, and that, my dear, directly."

" Oh, good gracious! "

" I shall take you the rounds."

" Visits! "

" Rectory, Patchpole, Rising-Proudly."

The Countess lay back.

" I wish to offend the Warristons," she said, " and Napier—and the gorgeous Mrs. Lampsacus. Oh, and a whole pack besides! "

" Napier has asked for you repeatedly—almost every day."

The Countess averted her face.

" I dare say," she said, " when he first heard of my marriage he was frightfully, frightfully upset? "

" Not so very. For five minutes he seemed inconsolably unhappy—and then he smiled! "

" Providentially! "

" Oh, my dear, you can't think how I've prayed for you all this while."

" Of course it's Catholicism now with both of us."

" It must be so strange."

" The child was baptized in Santa Maria in Cosmedin—she's been baptized twice, poor dear."

" For sake of ceremony? "

" At Santa Maria it was on account of *them*. It's their parish. But afterwards I took her round quietly and had it done in St. Peter's."

" You obtained your audience? "

" At the very last minute."

" Well! "

" Oh, well! I was prepared to do anything. Naturally! I'm sure! Oh, good gracious! "

" Was the child with you? "

" Oh, she waved her fat little wrinkled wrists—and smacked his Holiness—mother's Bianca did! My blessing! "

" As a family I gather you're inclined to be devout."

" Of course the dowager's goody. She never goes out without a string of nuns."

" Is there any reason for it! "

" I couldn't say. Often she'll kneel in the garden. Or on the stairs. Or in a shop. Or on a tram. Whenever she wants to she'll kneel! "

" She appears to be insatiable."

" It doesn't affect me. . . . On Sunday, as a rule, I've a box at the Argentina or a sofa stall at the Alcaza."

" Oio too? "

" Occasionally he comes."

" And when he doesn't! "

" There's always someone."

Mrs. Collins looked round.

" Wow! Here comes a big black doggie! "

" Daisy—my *dear! . . .*"

" Papa's waiting breakfast. He wants you to boil him an egg."

" Tell him I'll come."

" He's grumbling so. According to him, nobody cares at all whether he lives or dies. . . ."

Mrs. Collins raised a hand to her curls!

" Oh, poor granny! " she murmured as she withdrew.

Daisy subdued her ways.

" How did your little child sleep? " she asked.

" Well."

99

" Do you regret Rome? "

" It's a joy to have no mosquitoes! "

" That's not so bad as snakes. Suppose you had married an Indian."

" Thank goodness."

" Tell me about the Marriage State. Is it what you expected it to be? "

The Countess threw up her eyes.

" I didn't expect anything," she said.

" Let me look at your wedding-ring, Mabel, may I? Only for a minute."

" What do you want it for? "

" I won't eat it. "

" There's nothing very novel in a wedding-ring. Wait till you see my pearls? "

" Where are they ? "

" With my other jewels. . . ."

" I should like to borrow some."

" I dare say."

" Do you know of anyone likely to suit me? "

" A lover? "

" Nobody, Mab! . . ."

" I'm sorry."

" . . . Mabsey? "

" Oh, have *patience*."

" It's a pity the Bovon boys are so rabbity—they're for ever with their noses down a hole."

The Countess fluttered her eyelids.

" How are the dear ferrets? " she asked.

" All right."

" And the farm? "

" All right."

" Any changes? "

" Only in the house. Olga and Minnie have gone. Olga said she was glad to go. She said nothing would induce her to stop."

" Is Queen as queer as ever? "

" Queerer."

" Impossible."

" He and Mrs. Prixon don't get on. What Spicer endures at meals—talk about silence! And next week there'll be a fresh footman. It's funny the effect it always has upon me—it's something no one could explain! "

" In days gone by," the Countess said, " the pantry with a stranger in it was as dull as any drawing-room. . . ."

Daisy wriggled.

" Shall you ever forget the time Frank flew at you and clapped his hands? You were reaching for the pickled walnuts."

" Mercy! "

" And I was steadying the table for you as you got on it. Suddenly he . . . sprang."

The Countess looked vexed.

" Now you've scared the child."

" Oh, the poor wee sweetie! "

" Zito! Zito! Ah, Madonna!"

" I'll take her a turn in her little pram if she likes. Just the Aunt and the Niece together."

" Stay within call."

" We'll peep in the larder, shall we, Babs? There may be a bare birdie dangling there, and perhaps a little white corpse."

The Countess rang.

" Better wheel her under the yew-trees," she said, " out of the wind. And don't upset the pram! "

II

" WHEN the crow's-feet come
  And twirl about my eyes,
  And my lips turn pale . . .
  And my cheeks sink in,
  Oh, say, wilt thou love me then? "

Divorcing itself from the piano, the voice trailed magnificently away, ignoring altogether the tragical scepticism of the accompaniment.

The listeners looked shrewd.

Above the little party rose the Chase, dark and eerie in the autumn sun.

" Wilt thou love me truly when my hair has flown,
  When my teeth have fallen
  And my hands are wan?
  Oh, say, wilt thou love me then?

  I will love you (said he) for ever and ever,
  For ever and ever and ever and ever,
  Amen."

" Bis. Bis."

" It's the air from *Cunigonde*," Mrs. Collins explained, coming to the window.

" We were wondering what it was."

" In the death scene she introduces parts of it again in her delirium."

Mr. Collins frowned ferociously.

" Hag! " he muttered.

" By-and-by I will rattle you some of the ballet-music from *The Judgment of Paris*," the Countess said.

" Oh, the valse Paris sings—! He and the Three Graces. —Da-da-da-di-da! "

" If only the Chase were rid of! " Mrs. Collins complained.

" Has anyone been to view it? "

" Madame La Chose had the impudence to come. . . . Queen came to me one morning with the news that a lady with *an order* desired to see over the house. I guessed by his tone there was something extraordinary, and on going into the drawing-room there was Madame La Chose."

" Did you show her round? "

" Oh, my dear . . . yes. We even went so far as to fix some of the rooms."

" Mercy! "

" I must say I thought her rather charming."

" Would she care to take it? "

" Without the meadow she might. . . ."

" It shows her sense. Land nowadays is much too impoverishing."

" Her idea is to revive *Basset.* . . ."

" York being mainly a military town it would probably be a boon."

" In any case the decision, it seems, does not rest with herself alone, and she has asked to come back again."

" My dear, if she does . . .! " Mr. Collins said.

The Countess caressed her child.

" Mother, oh! . . . Poor mother, oh! Give a kiss to mother, oh! She says she *won't!* Oh, good gracious! . . ."

" I'm unhappy about her nurse," Mrs. Collins said. " A trustworthy person is everything."

The Countess crossed herself dejectedly.

" Oh, when I think of her nurses! . . ." she said. " At first I had a Roman one for the child. She was a regular contadina—La Marietta! La Mariuccia! But

she was so dirty! . . . A regular slut she was . . .
she wasn't even clean. And too *sans gêne,* by far. Bianca's
most impressionable. Nothing escapes her little eyes.
. . . So I sent her away and took a stranded Irish-
woman instead. Oh she was a terror. ' I always try to
please everybody,' she said, ' and I'm sorry I can't
you! ' But it was the tone of voice, dear, in which she
said it more than the actual words. . . . *Sapristi!*
However, one or two of them I liked. There was a
Swiss. . . . If she hadn't been so vague. One night,
my dear, she overturned the pram right in the middle
of the Corso! It might have killed the child. . . ."
"Are there no nice gardens that she could play
in?"
"There are. But it's a climb to get to them!"
"I'd an idea that Rome was flat. . . ."
Mr. Collins handled meditatively his cigar.
"What of the seven hills?"
"Ah, Charles!"
"Seven little hilly-willies!"
"I suppose the surrounding scenery is."
"You'd love Frascati. The land falls and rises, falls
and rises. Oh, it's ever so dear."
"I've a letter of yours from there."
"Did you keep the Greek ones?"
"I kept them all."
"I should like you to show me Gerald's."
Mrs. Collins looked away.
"Had I known the sort of woman she was! But
living as we do one never hears a thing."
"You had read her books."
"Ah, don't, Mabel."
"You liked her style."
"I'm told she's a noted Vampire."
"Who ever said so?"
"Some friend of hers—in Chelsea."
"What do Vampires do?"

" What don't they! "

" Of course she was always bizarre."

" Who could have foreseen her secret schemes?"

The Countess grew wan.

" Some of her literary secrets," she said, " were simply disgusting."

" Dissolute! "

" She'd force them from printers'-devils."

" Mabel."

" Was her last remarkable? "

" . . . The Londonisms! The Cockney! The slang!"

" She was a little too fond of her freedoms. . . ."

" Boys with their tutors. Girls with their mothers."

" According to you, Charles," Mrs. Collins said with umbrage, " I might be unwilling to chaperon the girls instead of fretting my life out in a hole like Bovon! "

Mr. Collins quelled the rising storm.

" There, Isabel," he said, with a glance towards the house, " if I thought we'd be here another summer I'd get new sun-blinds, dear . . . but what's the good? Just leaving them as fixtures."

III

" Queen," Daisy said to him one day. " If a fair young
gentleman with large blue eyes should call and ask for
Mrs. Collins you're to say she has gone out. . . .
But he'll find the Sisters in. The Aunt and the Niece
will be in the Yew-tree walk. With the Mother."

" Very good, miss."

" And, Queen——! "

" Fie, miss."

" Bashful? "

" I'm surprised."

The Yew-tree walk, the cause of so much gloom,
ran ring-like about the house, to meet again before the
drawing-room windows above the main road, where
a marble nymph with a worn flat face dispensed water,
rather meanly, out of a cornucopia into a trough full
of green scum.

On a garden swing near by the Countess was sway-
ing fitfully to and fro.

" Units, tens, hundreds, thousands. . . . Tens of
thousands. . . . Hundreds of thousands! *Units*——"
she was murmuring cryptically to herself with half
rapt looks.

" Shall I push you, Mabs? "

" No. Ta."

" To prevent the perspiration? . . ."

The Countess sighed.

" I'd sell my soul for an ice."

" A strawberry. . . ."

" Or vanilla."

" I told Queen we'd be in."

" Where's mum? "

" Upstairs. Trying on. It's the armpits again. . . ."
" Goodness! "
" Do you know the new snook, Mab? "
" Is there one? "
" A beauty."
" Not before Bianca."
" It's a pity the child's so young. . . ."
" Carissima! "
" Her little amours. Tell me about them. . . . Has she many? "
" She makes new conquests from day to day."
" Tell me things, Mabel."
" What things ? "
" All sorts of things."
" Really! "
" In Italy have they Brussels sprouts—like we have? "
" In Italy they've everything," the Countess replied.
" Can *he* speak English? "
" Fluently. Oh! . . ."
" Swear? "
" Certainly."
" A foreign husband wouldn't suit me—not if he stayed abroad."
" No? "
" Mabsey! "
" What is it ?"
" Nothing. In the afternoon the yew-trees turn quite blue."
" The quietness. . . . You can almost hear the clouds go by."
" Let's all lie down on the grass as if we were dead."
" It's too hot for rough games."
" I shouldn't wonder if it rained."
" Pitter-patter! "
" Every now and then she turns her great beseech-

ing eyes at me and whispers 'Aunt.' Aunt! she says, come back with me to Rome. Come! And let me have no nonsense now. Oh, Blanche, I reply . . . it's my poverty, dear. But what can one do on a penny a week? "

" Papa, poor-old-gentleman, was saying how you should be going to school."

" To school ? "

" That was what he said."

" He can't force me to if I choose to remain unlettered."

" It's for the companionship there'd be."

" Never."

" School isn't so dreadful, Daisy."

" Nothing would induce me to go."

The Countess rocked drowsily.

" At York Hill," she said, " looking back on it all, I seem to have enjoyed everything. Even the walks! Oh. . . . Often we'd go round the city walls . . . or along the Ouse perhaps out to Bishopsthorp and there we'd take the ferry. All we screaming girls and governesses in mid-river. . . . Oh, good gracious! "

" I remember the letters you sent from there. And the complaints that were in them! "

" And in the evening of course there'd be Preparation. . . . Oh—! That was always a time for mischief. . . . One of us, Annie Oldport perhaps ('Any-Old-Port' we used to call her), would give her next neighbour a squeeze, with orders to pass it on. How we did thrill when little Evelyn Rise, one of the new kids, took hold of the Principal herself. 'What are you doing to me, Evelyn?' 'I'm pinching you, Mrs. Whewell.' 'Are you indeed! Well, then——' And she dealt her a blow on the ears before us all. . . . Oh, Evelyn Rise! She was a little silly. . . . She hadn't any brains at all."

" No brains, Mabsey? "

" No," the Countess crooned. " She hadn't any."

" There! Queen's beckoning. . . ."

" Imbecile."

" It may be him."

" Who, him? "

" Your husband."

" Hardly."

" Your Excellency. . . ."

" Here I am."

" There's a person at the gate."

" Open it then."

" I fear it's a trouble."

" Why, who is it? "

" A stranger."

" It's perhaps the Count."

" It looks to be like a woman."

" The Sisters have gone away, Queen. . . ."

" Does she refuse her name? "

" Quite."

" A foreigner? "

" And *so* suspicious."

" The Aunt's away from home. . . ."

" I've often heard of the Black Hand, your Excellence, and lately I've noticed chalk-marks on the gate."

" *Ah, Dio!* "

" Is there no gentleman, Queen? "

" No, miss."

" It may be Jocaster Gisman."

" What Gisman? "

" The accomplice of Bessie Bleek that suffocated seven little boys and girls and was tried and executed for doing so. . . ."

" Oh, heavens! "

" Jocasta got herself off at the last Assizes—there were extenuating circumstances the judge said—and so he forgave her."

" *Bô!* "

" Mercy! "

" My dear, it's me," Miss Dawkins said, peering through the fence.

" That is so," she added, with an impetuous bound.

" Oh, the child! "

" Her aversion—I should say it's a flea," Miss Dawkins commented, subsiding upon the swing.

The Countess pushed it.

" Of all the surprises! " she said.

" I refused to give my name because it makes me cry to say it. I break down. . . ."

" You've not found them then? "

" No, dear."

" I imagined you in the I's."

" I sail for India within a week."

" The cathedral cities bring you north? "

" York and—they rhyme together . . . the first few letters. And I cling to every straw."

" Courage."

" Call me Ola."

" Ola."

" When I was in the Holy City I saw you one day."

" When was it? "

" During Passion Week."

" Were you with friends? "

" I scarcely knew anybody. I had an introduction to Countess Roderigos Samurez Dalmatia, but as I didn't like the look of her I didn't make use of it."

" I've heard of her often," the Countess said, " through the Grittis."

" Besides a letter to Princess Anna di Portici. . . ."

" Her house is occupied at present by the Marquesa Refoscosca! "

" And a card for Monsignor Ferrol."

" Old *débauché.*"

" Well . . . and how's the pleasant husband? "

" Oio? He's in Orvieto still. It's the Vintage. . . ."
Miss Dawkins looked devout.

" In my opinion," she said, " Orvieto wine is supe-
rior to the best Castelli."

" You should have a dozen, dear, of our Old-Old-
Old—the *Certosa*, if I knew where it would find you."

" I'm at the ' Wheat Sheaf.' "

" What? "

" Yes. I thought I'd repose myself there until I
start."

" If you've made no other plans you'll just stay
and rest with us until your ship sails."

" It's kind of you to ask me, but what will your
kindred say? "

" My dear, they'll love to have you. And mum will
tell you so herself. She's with the tailor now."

" It's the arm-pits! . . ."

" This is my little sister."

" And is that your babe? "

" Isn't she a darling! "

" Tell me, Contessa—have I changed since Greece?"

" I should say you're a little stouter."

" Ireland makes one sloppy."

" And I? . . ."

" My dear, you don't look fifteen."

" She's seventeen," Daisy said, " or thereabouts.
And the child will soon be two."

" Were *I* to have a child I should be just like a
lunatic," Miss Dawkins declared.

" With your tender heart I wonder you don't
marry."

" Marriages are made in heaven, you know."

" Let me find you someone! "

" You, my dear. . . . I've a sprig of the real
Chinduai charm-flower from the Malay. I've only to
wear it! "

" Why don't you then? "

" Voyagers lose their illusions somehow. . . . They lose them. . . ."

" Take off your hat and really rest! "

" Shall I? "

" Do."

" It's pretty peaceful here anyway," Miss Dawkins said, with a sigh, her eyes riveted upon the cornucopia of the niggardly nymph.

" Is it iron? " she inquired.

" What, the water? It's always rather brown. . . ." Miss Dawkins pressed a hand to her hip.

" It looks like a stream of brandy," she said, going off into a laugh.

I V

THE " intimate " dinner arranged by Mrs. Collins in honour of her daughter proved to be a large one.

A dinner of twenty at a table to hold eighteen.

As course succeeded course came the recurring pressure of a forward footman's knee.

Half asleep holding a shell-shaped spoon Miss Dawkins explored a sauce-boat as though it had been an Orient liner.

" Yes Mr. Collins."

" No Mr. Collins."

" Aha Mr. Collins."

(" *Thanks !*")

" Yes, God is Love, Mr. Collins, and I'm sure they couldn't help it! " she said at last.

" *Già! Già!* " the Countess struck in, allegro, across a bank of flowers.

" Well, here's health, old girl. The very best! "

" And success to you . . . and may the gods permit you to find them! "

" If you ask me, I think it silly to find people," the Countess's former inamorato declared. " I don't want to find anybody! . . ."

" No doubt you've tried clairvoyance? " the Member for Bovon asked.

" Indeed. And palmistry, and phrenology, and cards, and sand. . . ."

" Well? "

" Oh well . . ." Miss Dawkins said, " I was warned I'd marry a septuagenarian within the forbidden degrees and never know it! . . . Helios, Mene, Tetragrammaton! "

" Have you looked by the Rhine at all? "

" Where haven't I? "

" Courage! " the Countess crooned.

" I've a presentiment they're in India. Somehow I connect my mother's fair hair with Bombay. . . ."

Mr. Collins raised his glass.

" Then here's to Bombay! "

" Oh, nectar, Mr. Collins! Show me the cork—I always like to see the cork—! And my dear father was like me there. ' The cork, Ola,' he'd say. ' A bottle of wine is nothing without the cork.' "

" The Count! " Napier Fairmile with generosity proposed.

The Countess shrugged her shoulders.

" I'd a letter from Italy this morning," she said. " It appears in Rome all the roads are up."

" Up? "

" There's no getting by the Corso at all. Persons going to the Villa Borghese have to pass by the Via Babuino. Oh, good gracious! And my friend says the heat! It's a grill. Everyone is away still, of course, in villegiatura. But even so! At the Baths at Lucca she says she hears they're burning. . . ."

" Well, it was pretty warm, dear, in Greece," Miss Dawkins said. " The day of the accident I shall never forget how very hot it was! "

" At Salamis. . . ."

" Ah, don't."

" Was there ever such a misfortune? "

" There seems to have been some inexcusable carelessness."

" There are certain things we shall never know," the Countess murmured, " but I've sometimes thought that shot was aimed at me! "

Mrs. Collins shook her fan.

" The crazy people Mabel met in Greece! "

" Both Dorinda, Lady Gaiheart and Mrs. Arbanel

are parting from their husbands, so I understand."

" Poor Lady Dorinda! I fear she has fallen between two stools," the Member for Bovon said.

" And a piano. And a waste-paper basket, if reports are true," the Countess replied.

" Did you meet the Viviotts at all? "

" There was a Mrs. Viviott," Miss Dawkins said— " a nervy, pretty thing. She and a Mrs. Erso-Ennis. . . . Inseparable. And always quarrelling."

" They're reconciled again. And are gone to live at Birdingbury—quite near us—because it sounds Saxon..."

" Really, Viola? "

Mrs. Newhouse, *née* Neffal, nodded.

" Anything *fair!* " the Countess crooned. " Even a dancer."

" La Tasajara? I saw her one night. I believe it was at Astrea Fortri's house in Pall Mall. . . ."

" Such a little starved-soul ghost-face. Like a little thin-pale-pinched St. John," the Countess critically said.

" In the end she became indispensable to Miss O'Brookomore," Miss Dawkins stated.

" With Gerald? "

" Oh, that woman." Mrs. Collins shuddered.

" They tell me she's to chaperon an Eton boy straight to Tibet."

Miss Dawkins became abstracted.

" She evidently likes them young and fresh! " she observed.

The Countess started.

" What is it? " she asked.

" Come quickly! " her sister said. " The child's in her cups."

" Bianca is? "

" What have you been giving her? "

" It's only the little hiccoughs. . . ."

" Remember you weren't to come in till dessert."

"During the Stratford mulberries papa said I might. You've had them."

"Just look at her waist!"

"Now I'm here, mayn't I stop?"

"If you like to display your natural gifts," Mr. Collins murmured, "you may."

"You can't do much on an empty stomach."

"You can recite, I suppose," the Countess said.

"Recite? It's always an effort for me to recite. . . . I feel struck dumb in society."

"Remember Rome!" the Countess warned. "We've no use for shyness there."

"On his tombstone in the grass,
Record of him he was an ass,
He stretched out his neck and he flicked up his ears
And bid farewell to this valley of tears.

He lay himself down on a bed to die,
Right in a flower-bed himself he lay,
He stiffened his back and he whisked round his tail
And bid farewell to this earthly vale.

—On his tombstone in the grass,
Record of him he was an *Ass*."

"Charming!"

"How very, very, very, very vulgar!" the Countess frowned.

"Was it the devil, my dear?"

Mrs. Collins rose.

"Gentlemen," she murmured, "*à tout à l'heure!*"

"Let's all go into the garden, Mabsey."

"There's no moon."

"There are stars."

Miss Dawkins peered out.

"It's dark and like Gethsemane," she said.

[Chapter IV appears here as it stood in the edition of 1916.]

[Another, dated "Rome, April 1925," is now printed for the first time.]

I V

THE "intimate" dinner arranged by Mrs. Collins in honour of her elder daughter promised to be a large one. Covers for twenty guests, at a table to hold eighteen, insured nevertheless a touch of welcome snugness. In the crepuscular double drawing-room, commanding the eternal moors,* county society, as it assembled, exchanged cheery greetings. It was indeed to all intents the Doncaster Meeting lot.

Discanting away from homely topics, Sir Harry Ortop had just seen a fox, it seemed, crossing Cockaway Common, while Miss Rosalba Roggers had passed a traction-engine in the Rectory lane. " Horrid thing; but the Scarboro' road is really a disgrace," she pronounced, turning her attention to an angular beauty clad in sugary pink and a crown of birds' feathers.

Holding forth in a quizzical, hoarse-sweet voice, she was arraigning her husband with indescribable archness: " He always gets into his carriage first, and then half shuts the door on you! "

Momentous in his butlerhood, Queen, supported by an extra footman, announced each new advent with an air of serene detachment.

Mr. Napier Fairmile, Miss Nespole——

Entering on the heels of the former inamorato of the Countess sailed a mite of a woman enveloped fancifully in a fairy-hued cashmere shawl. The Cyclopean chatelaine of Cupingforth Castle, and one of the wealthiest women in the Riding, she was held, by local

* "Finely situated on the edge of the moors."—*Vide* Estate Agents' Announcements.

117

opinion, to be eccentric for preferring to live all alone, which may possibly have had its dangers for a person of her condition and sex; nevertheless, on occasion, to convince an intrusive stranger she had a male in the house, she would discharge a cartridge out of window, and knot her hair across her chin in front in a thick cascade to imitate *a beard*.

Lady Watercarriage, The Hon. Viola West-Wind, Captain Margaret-Baker——

Quite re-vitalised, performing her duties, Mrs. Collins circulated smilingly here and there. Throwing a veil of glamour upon each guest, she had introduced Miss Dawkins twice as " The Great Traveller."

" I ain't going back to Australia not yet awhile. That is so!" Miss Dawkins declared, recognising across the Rector's shoulder in the damp-stained mezzotints upon the walls some views of popular thoroughfares her foot had trodden—Trafalgar Square, the Place de la Concorde, the Piazza Colonna, the Puerta del Sol. " If I don't just spit at them! " she commented, idly opening and closing her fan.

The Farquhar of Farquhar, Mrs. Lampsacus of Gisborough Park——

Already a full quarter-of-an-hour late, they were yet not the last.

Masticating, chewing the air, Mr. Collins appeared to have become involved against his will in the esoteric confidences of a pair of expansive matrons: " In York I saw some very pretty . . . I enquired the price. . . . Would you believe . . . *Need* I say I bought them!"

Delivered from their effusive unbosoming by The Farquhar of Farquhar, Mr. Collins turned away.

Advancing like some marvellous automaton, The Farquhar, known as " Lulu " to all frequenters of the Turf, brought with him an atmosphere of one who had supplied a daughter, or at least a filly, to a Prince of the Blood. Excusing his wife Serafima (a woman for whom undergraduates had shot themselves), he inquired, with a leer, for " la petite Comtesse."

She was looking summery and semi-Southern in an imaginative gown in every shade of white.

" Precious darling! She's only eight months; it's a critical age," she was exclaiming; apropos, doubtless, of her child.

Chatting to a bottle-nosed dowager in garnets and goose-flesh, she appeared indeed even prettier than she was.

Descending on her, The Farquhar was circumvented by Miss Viola West-Wind, a young girl of the County with a little Tatler-tainted face. She was supplying blocks of tickets, it seemed, for *The League of Patriots* ball . . . " *Fancy dress! Everyone to go as animals.*"

Dr. Dee——

It was as much as to say dinner; but an announcement, breathed from Queen, was to fill Mrs. Collins with apprehension.

" There's been a little catastrophe, 'm."

" What, not . . . ? . . . ! . . .? ? "

" To a cinder, 'm."

In the long low-ceiled dining-room, all in the robust mid-Victorian style, the failure of an *entrée* seemed a more or less trivial thing; in such an environment it is the haunch that matters, it is the loin that tells. . . .

" Even so," Mrs. Collins heard herself murmuring (almost callously) as she gained a chair on The Farquhar's arm—" Even so. The mornings begin to be frosty."

A random word wafting the talk naturally to the subject of foxes.

" Count Pastorelli is fond of hunting? "

But Mrs. Collins presumed a prudent deafness.

Adorned with foreign spring flowers, smart jonquils and early tulips, the table-arrangements left nothing to be desired.

" I could never go to Russia; I turn quite green in the snow," Miss Dawkins was telling Sir Harry Ortop of her Odyssey.

" I take it you've tried clairvoyance?" he asked.

" Indeed. And palmistry, and phrenology, and cards, and sand. . . ."

" Well? "

" Oh well . . ." she replied, regarding a scar on his third blue chin; " I was warned I'd marry a septuagenarian within the forbidden degrees and never know it. . . . Helios, Mene, Tetragrammaton! "

" According to my experience, it's a mistake to find people. I don't want to find anybody. . . ."

Miss Dawkins used her fan.

" I've a presentiment they're in India," she said. " Somehow I connect my mother's fair hair with Bombay. . . ."

Owing to the absence of a guest, it was agreeable to find the Countess in juxtaposition. With the Member for Bovon on her right, her tongue tripped heedlessly from Mussolini to Miss Anne : " Poor soul, she was interred in her lace, with a coin of Greece in her mouth, and a flask of Chalkis wine, and a tambourine."

A version of the Salamis affair that was new to Miss Dawkins.

" ——! " she cooed, lifting her eyes in protest to a painting of Mary Marchioness of Jamaica and Miss Elizabeth Cockduck, of the school of Sir Thomas Lawrence.

" . . . just as in the Golden Age; and the moon that night was extra enormous," the Countess broke off her tale, arrested by a wail of distress from the direction of the nursery.

The notion that Daisy might be diverting herself at Bianca's expense caused the Countess to rise.

" Precious darling! *C'est l'heure du berger* for the

child," she exclaimed, directing her steps towards the door.

Traversing the hall, she perceived Daisy in the morning-room examining the visitors' wraps; lifting the fabrics to her nose (much as might a savage), she appeared to be voluptuously revelling in the human odours they exhaled.

" Fie, girl! What are you up to?" her sister asked.

" The Farquhar of Farquhar's muffler, Mabel, has such a funny smell, something between honey and flowers and new goloshes."

" Oh! "

" And Lady Watercarriage's cloak! I don't know what it is, but it's almost overpowering."

" *Santo dio*," the Countess breathed, lending an ear to the uproar above.

Daisy displayed indifference.

" She's overturned her little Tamara again, I suppose, that's all! ! ! !"

In the shadowy nursery, bafflingly lit by the dancing stars, some romantic fancy, it seemed, had disquieted the child.

On beholding both Mother and Aunt with a radiant light, she crowed, she smiled.

" Bianca . . . Mother's heaven." The Countess hovered.

" From the look in those endless eyes of hers I shouldn't wonder if she hadn't seen the Owl that lived in an Oak.

> There was an owl lived in an oak—
> Whiskey, waskey, weedle;
> And every word he ever spoke
> Was fiddle, faddle, feedle."

" Don't, Daisy! "

" Oh, she loves her little Buen Retiro (when it's dry); her own private corner in Bedfordshire."

" Let her be," the Countess answered, availing herself of the opportunity to deck with fresh white and red her constantly piquant face.

" Has anyone cast a doubt on your union, Mab, being legal?" Daisy asked, surveying with the eyes of a retired bus-horse her sister's comfortable back.

" Don't ask silly questions, Daisy, if you don't want foolish answers," the Countess returned, following in the mirror her infant's yearning glance towards a bespangled negro doll, Topolobampa, Queen of the Sunset Isles.

·" 'Cos I s'pose you know that's what Spicer's been tellin' George. . . ."

" George?"

" The extra footman."

" Oh, good gracious!"

" Naturally he'll repeat it. It seems he goes all over Yorkshire waiting, but his home-proper is the Capital. Hull, he says, is a dreadful place. No season, and with the morals of Sodom. And, fancy, Mabsey, his brother is the boy from Willinghorse and Wheelits. . . ."

" What!"

" He aspires to the concert hall, he says, on account of his voice. So we made him sing and I must say his rendering of ' Early one morning before the sun was dawning ' won all our hearts."

The Countess shrugged.

" She wants, I think, to take Topolobampa to bed!" she irrelevantly exclaimed.

" She'd rather take her old Aunt—eh, chubby?"

" Madonna, what next!"

" Her little body, Mab . . . it's as soft as satin ! Oh, it's terrible!"

" —— . . . ?"

" How arch the puss looks in her little nainsook!"

" Mind and don't tease her, Daisy," the Countess enjoined as she frisked away.

An odour of meat, wine and flowers hung erotically upon the dining-room air.

"I want my life to be purple—— Never less," Miss Dawkins was assuring the Member for Bovon.

Curtailing their colloquy, the Countess resumed her place.

At a delicate advantage with her newly-geraniumed lips, she was in a mood to enjoy herself.

"Look two to your right; who is she, Countess?" Miss Dawkins asked.

"An immense heiress! Miss Nespole of Cuping-forth."

"My dear, she's the most extraordinarily-looking woman that I ever set eyes on!" Miss Dawkins serenely stated.

Taking umbrage from her stare, Miss Nespole (with the eccentricity permitted to wealth) put out her tongue at her and drew it slowly in again.

"Oh, good gracious!" the Countess exclaimed, shooting a glance towards her father.

Listening to a description of Gleneagles from Lady Watercarriage, he appeared almost to have grown into his chair.

"And from there we went on to a ghastly hotel where *all the bedclothes are grey,*" the peeress fluted, fingering the pearls on her forward-falling shoulders.

The Countess raised a discreet glass of Perrier to her lips.

But as course succeeded course The Farquhar was moved to beg his hostess to allow her younger daughter to join them for the sugared kickshaws at dessert.

A lover of young girls and with a cult for them, he was believed to harbour Satanesque inclinations towards the Age of Candour.

"Just for a prune!" he insidiously pressed, brushing a napkin to the spreading branches of his moustache.

123

Miss Dawkins, meanwhile, was becoming blandly Bacchic.

" Oh, thank you, Member for Bovon, sweetest of men to me," she exclaimed, addressing him champagnishly across her friend.

It was towards the close of dessert, just as the ladies were about to withdraw, that Daisy, clasping Bianca, chose to present herself. " I brought Niece, too; I thought it would widen her little sphere," she chirruped, coming blithely forward into the room.

She had a coronet-brooch on a well trussed-out blouse, and a strip of deep green velvet tied sparkishly below the middle.

Cautioned by her sister's eye, she turned towards the Rector, who was engaging to loan a stallion to a parishioner. " A thing I seldom do," he murmured, bestowing a frigid smile on the infant papist.

Refusing to wet her lips in some curaçoa, Daisy approached The Farquhar. Appreciating notice, his jolly ogle was a welcome stimulus.

A blood-orange? Grapes? . . . Preserve-of-ginger? She answered him whimsically by a little leap of the tongue.

" She's an amusette, Mrs. Collins, your wee girl; a sweet piece; ah, these golden blondes! . . . these golden blondes!"

" But why is that? " Mrs. Collins inattentively answered, watching her grandchild circulate, as might a fruit, from guest to guest along the table.

Flattered by The Farquhar's interest, Daisy was demonstrating already her social acumen.

" I've seen statues . . . often. Oh it's terrible!" she rapported, shooting back her hair.

" Little deviless! Where? " the Farquhar queried, stealing a surreptitious arm about her middle.

" Often on lawns, and in gardens, too; oh it's terrible! "

" . . . Indeed," he murmured, alarmed by an ear-piercing shriek, attesting to Bianca's aversion to the Rector.

It was a warning, it seemed, to adjourn. Laughing hectically as she rose, Miss Dawkins had lost her bearings.

"Where ever was I last old October?" she exclaimed, waving the long lyric feathers of her fan in Sir Harry Ortop's face. "I'll own I forget. . . ."

V

" Yes, dear, and so I'm really off—! And there were
so many things I had wanted to say to you. But somehow I've not found time."

" Stay another week," the Countess begged.

" Call me Ola."

" Ola."

" Your father's a regular rake, darling."

" What are you looking for? "

Miss Dawkins gazed with lethargy about the room.

Above the mantelpiece were engravings of Sa-
lammbô in Matho's tent and Monna Vanna in Prinzi-
valle's, known collectively as *The Fair Trespassers*, and
published by the Fine Art Society " as the Act directs."

" The Isol," she said.

" I love your box, Ola."

" It's not distinguished."

" The labels it has on it! "

" Driving to and from a place in carnival time the
students take it away."

" I envy you your independence."

" I'd rather roost."

" Domesticity tires one so. Every time I enter the
nursery now it's a strain. To-day was the climax. I've
had many years' experience, Mrs. Occles said to me,
as a nurse, and I'll have no meddling. Very well, I
said to her, you can go! Oh, good gracious! Then at
the door, dear, I turned back and I added, Am I the
child's mother or are you? That, she said, is no affair
of mine! But as a rule I'm accustomed to see the
father! ! What do you mean by the father? I said.
But she wouldn't say."

Miss Dawkins passed her parasol beneath the bed.

" My button boots——! "

" A child has so many little wants, nurse, I said. . . .
It should have proper attention. . . . *I* know what
a child wants, she said (so rudely), and when it wants
it. . . . And there was Bianca looking at her with her
little eyes. . . ."

" Still, I wish the Count would come! "

"I hope he's not false to me," the Countess quavered.

" Foreigners usually are, dear. They deceive their
wives. . . ."

" If I thought he was unworthy. . .?"

" You're sure, of course, it's binding ?"

" Binding? "

" No loopholes? "

The Countess tittered.

" None," she said.

" Knowing the world as I know it," Miss Dawkins
sighed. " Ah, well. . . ."

" There . . . the carriage is at the door."

" I'm ready."

" Have you a magazine or anything for the train? "

" I've a novel only—*Three Lilies and a Mouſtache.*"

" I like a love ſtory," the Countess confessed, " so
long as it isn't drivel."

" Here is Daisy to say good-bye."

" Where's Niece? "

" In France! " the Countess crooned.

" Isn't the child here? "

" Come and kiss me," Miss Dawkins invited.

" I've such news! "

" What is it? "

" The Chase is let at laſt."

" Goodness! "

" Madame La Chose is in the library now with a
professional witness."

" Well? "

" And they've taken the house. I was listening. . . .
Madame La Chose said she was prepared to put her
hand to an agreement for a ninety-nine years' lease
without the farm. And it's to be pulled down immediately. . . . Oh, the rats! "

" Who's the witness? "

" General Lover."

" My dear father once struck me for listening at a
door," Miss Dawkins observed.

" And as a reference she gives La Belle Zula. She says
her diamonds *alone* are worth the half of Yorkshire."

" Mum must be overjoyed."

" She is."

" One place or another! " Miss Dawkins drawled.
" Once the glamour's gone."

" Oh, Ola! "

" I maintain there's little in it."

" I long to go about! " Daisy murmured, pirouetting vainly before the glass.

" Jesu! "

" What openings have I here? "

" There's time enough yet," the Countess assured.

" One sister should help another."

" When you're eligible we'll see."

" If I'm not eligible now I don't know who is! "
Miss Dawkins drew on nervously a glove.

" You've my address in Australia, Viscountess, all
right? "

" Belleview—isn't it? Lake George? . . ."

" That's it, old girl."

" I shan't forget."

"I hope the sea'll be level, dear. I can't endure it rough."

" Write soon."
Miss Dawkins nodded.

" It depends on the Master Potter now. But if I
ever should find my beloved ones in the East I'll be
sure to let you know."

VI

" How would Phryne Street appeal to you, Isabel? "
Mr. Collins asked his wife as they sat one morning at
breakfast.

" H-m, Charles! . . ."

" Maxilla Gardens then? "

" H-m! . . ."

" Or Gardingore Gate? "

" I want to live in Lisbon," Mrs. Collins said.

Mr. Collins cast aside the paper.

" Where to bend our footsteps to is a problem and
a tragedy," he muttered.

" 'Vieto," Daisy suggested in an insinuating voice.

" What would one do dumped down in Orvieto? "
Mrs. Collins asked. " It would be as bad as Bovon."

" At 'Vieto it's all arcades, and right on top of a hill!
You've to take a lift to get to it. It's the funicular for
all. . . ."

" If it's to be Italy I'd sooner it was Rome."

Daisy showed fervour.

" Mab was telling me of the preserves they sell
there. All speared on little sticks. At the street corners,
she says, the sugar-plums sparkle in the sun just as if
they were jewels. . . . I should like to see them. . . .
And to taste them too," she added.

" Papa has written to Mrs. Whewell already, alas,"
Mrs. Collins said, " to inquire whether she has a vacancy
at all at York Hill."

" If I studied anywhere it would be abroad."

" Master your native tongue at any rate to begin
with," Mr. Collins advised.

" I don't care a jot for distinctions! "

" At your age," Mrs. Collins asserted, " I had a
diploma."

" For what? "

" As a nurse."

" Nursing's different."

" I assure you it's very disagreeable. Often it's by
no means pleasant."

" Why? "

" What I never could bear about nursing," Mrs.
Collins reminiscently said, " was sponging the paint
off the face of a corpse."

" I would leave it."

" Even a hospital nurse can go too far. . . ."

" Where's Mabel? "

" I heard her romping with Bianca as I passed her
door."

" She doesn't bother herself much of a morning
about the time," Mr. Collins complained.

" It's on account of prayers, Charles. Until they're
over she naturally doesn't care to come down."

Daisy sipped her tea.

" She did her best to convert me the other day,"
she said. " With one of her hatpins."

" What? "

" . . . An old bead affair. Such a common thing.
Not worth sixpence."

" Mab did? "

" And she has her eye on Queen! "

" I fear the tap-room at the Mitre is as near as *he'll*
ever get to Rome," Mr. Collins remarked.

" S-s-s-h, Charles. Here he is! "

" Is the Signora stirring yet, Queen? " Daisy asked.

" She has just received her letters."

" Is there anything for me? "

" No, Miss Daisy. There is not."

" I was only wondering——"

Mrs. Collins raised a hand.

" Hark! "

" O-o-o-o-o-o-h! "

" It's her ladyship's cry."

" You'd think Great Pan was dead again—at least."

" Very likely it's her husband's handwriting that affects her," Daisy said. " Or it may be only a parcel! She's expecting, on approval, I know, some fancy-work pyjamas."

" O-o-o-o-o-o-h! "

" Breakfast! " Mrs. Collins carolled.

" He's coming. He'll be here to-day," the Countess announced, elated. " Oio will! "

" Positively? "

" So he says. Oh. . . . And in the night I was dreaming so vividly of a runaway hearse. . . . As it galloped by me one of the mourners gave me *such* a look. I can see it now."

" Was it anybody, Mabsey? "

" How anybody? "

" Likely to suit me."

" A husband! "

" Mabsey! "

" It was a young woman. . . . Poor soul!" the Countess replied.

" What does he say? "

" I'll read you out some of his letter. But it isn't all for you."

" Is it in Italian, Mabel? "

" It's half and half."

" Well? "

" ' My dear dearly,' he begins—he always calls me *dearly!*—' My own, own, little wife. My Mabina——' And then he simply says he's coming. ' *Spero di venire Sabato verso la sera.* . . .' And he sends his filial love, with a kiss, to the English mother—à la mamma Inglese. . . ."

" Ah? "

" Yes. . . . And he intends to take her back with him to Italy, where he has prepared for her benefit a violet and rose salotto. . . ."

" Bless the boy! "

" And then there's a piece of scandal. Oh, good gracious! . . . He says poor Citta Zocchia isn't to wait on the Queen any more! She's done it *this* time. . . . And Dona Formosa de Bergère is to be married in Naples—*Naples!* Oh! Mercy!—to a certain Signor Popi! . . ."

" At what o'clock will he be here? "

" *Verso la sera!* "

" What time would that be? "

" Towards night."

" How vague these husbands are."

" He'll be here for dinner, I dare say," Daisy said.

" We must try to consult his tastes."

" Simple, nourishing things," the Countess said, " he likes. He has a passion for curry."

Mrs. Collins concealed her anxiety.

" In Rome, for example, Mab," she asked, " what do they have when they dine? "

" It depends."

" Besides curry . . ."

" Oh, well, perhaps some little round, pink, sweet potatoes they'll have, and some plain stewed rice. Or, again, very likely it'll be a piece of cold pickled pork. With olive oil and onions. . . . Whatever's seasonable they'll have. . . . And on Friday, of course, it's *fish.*"

" You'll need to tell all this presently to Mrs. Prixon," Mrs. Collins said. " And don't forget one thing. . . . You've to replace that Mrs. Occles."

The Countess sighed.

" If I can't be suited with a Bovon girl or a York young thing I shall have an ayah and get the baby used to things. . . ."

Daisy raised a finger.

" There's her little howl! "

" Poor mite. She can't bear to be left alone with a strange Scotch woman. When Bianca takes an aversion! . . . She's a peculiar child in many ways."

" Let me dress her to-day, Mabsey, may I—just for once? "

" What ever for? "

" Leave her to me. I'll turn her out what's what! "

" Goodness! "

" I've my secrets. . . ."

" I dare say."

" I can build her quite a presence. . . ."

" Mercy! "

" With a proper projection you wouldn't know the child."

" I must fly to her."

" And do, dear, finish your toilet," Mrs. Collins beseeched.

" I trust her husband will confiscate all her trailing, bedraggled negligeys," Mr. Collins said. " Slovenly, nasty things! "

Daisy rippled.

" I wouldn't build upon it," she replied. " Her husband often doesn't get up himself in the morning at all."

" Not? "

" He lies a-bed until all hours. He's a regular sluggard. The shadows will be falling sometimes, she says, and daylight almost gone, and you'll find him still between the sheets."

" Fortunately Madame La Chose will be routing us out of this before very long."

" Eh, Is-a-bel! "

Mrs. Collins glowed.

" And what heavenly happiness," she remarked, " to have no housekeeping—ever any more! "

" Let's all dance to-night."

" My madcap fairy! "

" Her husband dances quite wonderfully, she says."

" Who would there be to play? "

" Victoria owns a concertina."

" That's no good."

" And William has a banjo. . . . According to him, the banjo is the king of instruments."

" Nonsense. I shouldn't think it was."

" Oh! Mumsey! . . ."

" We might perhaps call in the Bovon string quartet," Mrs. Collins said. " Just for a serenade."

" Oh! what ever has happened to Niece? "

" If she's peevish, poor mite," the Countess said, returning, " it's on account of the little mulligrubs. . . ."

" You can't expect a child of her years to be reasonable," Mrs. Collins commented. " It wouldn't be natural."

" Let me have her," Daisy begged.

" Don't, Daisy! "

" What the child likes best is a reel of cotton. She'll play with that when she wouldn't play with me. . . ."

" *Pucci! Pucci!* " Mrs. Collins ventured.

" *Ecco la nonna! La buona cara nonna.* . . . Ah, *santo Dio!* "

" When I say *cui* to her, somehow she doesn't seem to like it! "

Daisy wagged her tongue.

" Lat-lat! "

" How can you be so gross! "

" Let me lull her. Shall I? "

" She's never quiet for you."

" Wait till she hears the story of Blowzalinda and the Fairy Bee."

" Oh, it's beyond the child. . . . She wouldn't know. Buz-z-z! "

" Isabel! "

" Yes, dear? "

" Cook requires her orders."

" Where is she? "

" Behind the screen."

" Help me, Mabel," Mrs. Collins said.

" *Gigi! Ribu!* Oh, the clim pickle! "

" Give her to me, Mabsey."

" Yum. Yum."

" Give her to me."

" She lifts her little hand up to her little nose and then she presses it."

" It's one of her little sarcasms, I expect."

" She finds the world *so* weird."

" Still it's good to know she has such an aunt. A good aunt, she says, is an untold blessing."

" Help me! " Mrs. Collins implored.

" How? "

" Curry—and then? . . ."

The Countess turned her head.

" He can't endure a rabbit," she remarked.

" My dear, no one proposes it! "

" Once the child and I were driving on the Via Appia Nuova when we saw a bunny peeping out of a tomb. Oh, such a darling! So I stopped the carriage and told Luigi, the footman, to run and dispatch it if he possibly could. He brought it back to me. . . . And a few hours afterwards it was bubbling away into a fine chicken broth. Oio had it all. . . . But hardly had it passed his lips when he was seized with the most violent spasms. Whereupon he turned round and accused me of attempting to do what certain Renaissance wives are supposed to have sometimes done. Oh! He was so cross. He was as cross as cross. . . . So don't let's have rabbit."

" Polpettino, perhaps? "

" In olive oil; garnished ' Mussolini-wise.' "

" And then? "

" Oh, then, what he really adores, what he simply can't resist, is a fritter."

" Cheese? "

" Any kind. And he loves a savoury! Zuccata, he likes. Zuccata, Zuccatini. . . . And he's fond of a soufflé too, so long as it isn't *led*."

" Not to anticipate, my dear . . ."

" Then——"

" Olive oil! "

" And then——"

" Then," Mrs. Collins' voice rose as if inspired, " then Côtelettes—à la Milanaise. . . ."